THe bROKen SPeLL

Also by Erika McGann:

The demon notebook

THE bROKen SPeLL

eRiKa mcGann

sourcebooks
jabberwocky

Published by Sourcebooks Jabberwocky, an imprint of Sourcebooks, Inc.
P.O. Box 4410, Naperville, Illinois 60567-4410
(630) 961-3900
Fax: (630) 961-2168
www.jabberwockykids.com

Originally published in 2013 in the United Kingdom by The O'Brien Press, Ltd.

Library of Congress Cataloging-in-Publication data is on file with the publisher.

Source of Production: Versa Press, East Peoria, Illinois, USA
Date of Production: September 2014
Run Number: 5002238

Printed and bound in the United States of America.
VP 10 9 8 7 6 5 4 3 2 1

*For my big brother, Oisín,
for being a much better writer than I'll ever be,
and really taking the pressure off.*

contents

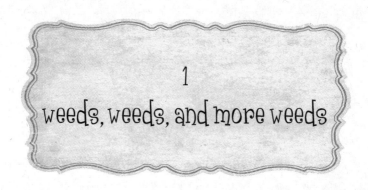

1
weeds, weeds, and more weeds

The demon's eyes, fiery red in the darkness, narrowed to slits as its almighty roar shook the world around them. Grace's straight, brown hair shone in the moonlight, cascading down the black silk cloak that billowed in the howling wind. Gripping the ruby-encrusted dagger in her right hand and raising it above her head, she took one fleeting look at the surrounding forest. They were there, the four shadows that confirmed her friends were strategically hidden among the trees.

"Your time has come," the demon growled, thick saliva dripping from its elongated fangs. "I'll devour your still-beating heart, and all your power will be mine!"

"Come and get it, demon!" shouted Grace.

The creature's claws curled tight as it sprang forward, missing Grace by inches as she dodged to the right. Screeching in frustration, the demon threw itself toward her feet, missing again as Grace leaped impossibly high into the air and hovered. Her cloak spread wide in the night sky before she dove to the ground and plunged the dagger deep into the demon's chest. Its horrible screams echoed throughout the woods, but with superhuman strength, Grace kept her grip on the hilt of the knife. The demon's claws encircled Grace's throat, squeezing and cutting into her skin.

"Foolish girl," it croaked. "You're mine now."

Grace hissed in agony, but leaned on the dagger, pushing it farther and farther into the monster's flesh. A sudden flash of reflected moonlight signaled the cavalry—Grace's four friends, Jenny, Rachel, Una, and Adie. Their silver ropes wrapped around the demon's wrists, pulling the creature away from Grace's neck toward the ground. The demon, spread wide with each of its tethered limbs held by one of the girls, writhed pathetically before lying still. Then Grace stood slowly and pulled the dagger from the demon's lifeless body. The creature's remains vanished in a puff of black smoke.

"He nearly had you then," Rachel said, her porcelain brow creased with worry.

Grace glanced at her own reflection in the dagger's blade and smiled.

"Nope," she drawled. "His heart wasn't in it."

"*Grace!* Are you paying attention?"

"Huh?" Grace snapped out of her daydream. She was back in Mrs. Quinlan's kitchen, with its musty cat smell and the misshapen piece of timber, perched on the counter and painted black, that served as a homemade blackboard. Grace squinted at the chalky diagrams of plants whose names she couldn't remember.

"Well?"

"Yes, Mrs. Quinlan."

"Good. Then wake up what's-her-face. She's drooling on my table."

Grace looked down at Una, who had fallen asleep

with her cheek directly on the worm-eaten wood. She gave her friend a firm, but gentle, pinch in the ribs.

"Wha—?"

Una shot upright, smacking her lips and wiping her mouth with her sleeve. Strands of her short, black bob stuck to her face, framing her gray eyes. She groaned.

"Did I miss anything good?"

"No," Adie said flatly. "Just more weeds."

Una rested her chin in her hands as her eyes drifted shut again, snapping open as Mrs. Quinlan cracked the board with her pointer in emphasis. The woman glared accusingly with her pale eyes and grimaced, showing off her yellowing teeth.

"And that's *really* important. Make sure you get that part down. Well, that's obviously all the information your pea brains are going to absorb today, so I guess you can get lost as soon as you like."

The girls rose to their feet like arthritic elderly ladies and mumbled insincere thank-yous.

"You *should* be thankful. No one's paying me for this, you know."

✳✳✳

"Do you remember doing photo-singdingding last year in science class?" said Una as the girls clambered through the wiry hedge that separated Mrs. Quinlan's street from the school grounds.

"Photosynthesis," corrected Grace. "And, yeah."

"Remember how we said it was the most boring class ever?"

"Yeah."

"Well, we were wrong. This is the most boring class ever. I can't feel my face I'm so bored. How is this so *boring*? I mean, it's supposed to be magic, so why is it *so* boring?" she paused. "*I'm so bored!*"

"Yes, we get that, Una, and you're not the only one," Jenny replied, her purple Doc boots stamping through the grass. "We're *all* bored. Who knew learning magic was mostly stupid botany and stuff? I mean, when you read about it online and check out the books, it's just all spells and curses and enchantments."

"I'd give my right arm to cast a good spell," sighed

Rachel. Her manicured nails plucked absently at a badge with a pentagram symbol hanging off the back of Jenny's backpack.

"We tried that before, remember?" said Grace. "Una got possessed by a demon, and we wound up with nine horrible spells to deal with? It wasn't exactly the best of times."

"Are you saying you're enjoying *this*?" Una's voice rose.

"No, I'm just saying that I get why we have to learn all the boring stuff first. I mean, it makes sense."

"Yeah, but it's *agony*!"

The tired silence that followed confirmed everyone's agreement. As they trundled across the football field, Grace's mind drifted back to her daydream of the demon in the woods and an enchanted ruby dagger.

✳✳✳

When the initial shock of their first adventure into the supernatural had worn off—and Una had recovered from being possessed by a demon—the five girls had been eager to continue with their lessons in witchcraft. Ms. Lemon had promised that she and Mrs. Quinlan would tutor them in magic, giving them all the tools they needed to keep themselves and others safe from the demon well. They were to become bona fide witches. This summer had promised to be the most exciting, adventurous summer of all time! But within two minutes of Mrs. Quinlan's first class, they knew it wasn't going to be—not by a long shot.

"There," Mrs. Quinlan had said, heaving a giant tome onto the kitchen table. "Learn that."

"What?" said Jenny. "The whole thing? What is it?"

"*Madame Papillon's Guide to Herbs and Weeds*, tenth edition. Updated to include the newest, most exciting discoveries from South America and Japan."

Grace blew some dust from the cover and opened the first page. "It was printed in 1910."

"For magic, that's new."

"Do we get to try out a spell today?" asked Una.

"No," replied Mrs. Quinlan. "You learn this first."

"Do we get to try spells as we're learning it?"

"No."

"Just little spells?"

"No."

"Can't we do a spell using a herb or weed when we've learned *all* about that herb or weed?"

"Yeah, sure."

"Really?" Una's face brightened.

"No."

"There's just so much of it," Grace murmured as she thumbed through the yellowed pages of delicate drawings and tiny text.

"Lesson number one," said Mrs. Quinlan, dragging her homemade blackboard off the floor and balancing it on the kitchen counter. "Witchcraft is all about *knowledge*. When a witch has knowledge, she has power. A powerful witch controls the spells she casts. A power*less* witch is controlled *by* the spells she casts. An obvious example is when you all cast a bunch of spells, willy-nilly, and nearly got dead for your trouble. *Learn* first. Magic later. So, what is lesson number one?"

She didn't wait for an answer but scrawled, with her nails occasionally scratching the board with teeth-clenching squeaks, *Knowledge = Power*.

"Write that in your notebooks in big capital letters," she said sternly. "It is by far the most important thing you will ever learn in this class."

The hour and a half that followed was full of Latin names, common names, domestic properties, supernatural properties, classification, location, identification… At the end of the class, Mrs. Quinlan smiled and said, "You may find it dull now, but when you've learned all the flora, we move on to—"

"Spells?" Una said, grinning.

"No, *fauna*. That's when things *really* get interesting. All right, class dismissed. That means get lost."

Every one of Mrs. Quinlan's classes so far had lived up to the excitement of the first. Hours and hours of pointless facts and sketching little leaves that all looked the same. Ms. Lemon's classes were marginally better. Always an enthusiastic teacher, she tried to inject some fun into the proceedings. They took field trips into the woods, where the girls would compete to identify lists of plants, winning glitter-filled pens and chocolate if they were fast enough. Sometimes she would take them to the beach and they would collect different types of seaweed and ancient coral leaf, if they could find it. She told them stories about the old days when she and Mrs. Quinlan were at school together, and about all the spells of theirs that had gone wrong, and why.

"It's a very fine art," she said. "There are so many ingredients, so many combinations, so many ways for it to go wrong. But when you know your way around magic, the possibilities are endless."

"We wouldn't know," grumbled Rachel.

"Patience, girls," Ms. Lemon said, tapping Rachel on the nose with a dried piece of seaweed. "Good things come to those who wait."

The girls had waited. Three whole months of hard work with no end in sight. By the time September came around, they were almost looking forward to school starting.

"Good morning, class," said Mr. Collins loudly, striding into Grace, Adie, and Rachel's geography class, and not waiting for the kids to settle down. "I'm afraid Mr. Gains will not be returning this year. As I'm sure you've all heard, he had a very unfortunate, and frankly bizarre, gardening accident. I am sure we will all think twice before balancing on rickety patio furniture while using an electric hedge trimmer. But, on to happier things. To replace Mr. Gains, we have a new geography teacher joining us. Ms. Gold." He gestured toward the door and the new teacher entered.

Ms. Gold could not have been more aptly named. She beamed brightly, her hand brushing her shoulder as she swept back long locks of golden blond hair that glistened in the morning sunshine. Her eyes were such a light shade of brown they also appeared golden. Even her skin had a luminosity that seemed to light up the whole room.

"Wow," Adie whispered. "She's *so* pretty." She frowned, tucking away a few dark curls that had escaped from her hair tie. Her almond-shaped eyes gazed enviously at the lovely woman standing next to Mr. Collins.

"Wonder if that's a foundation, or just a moisturizer," Rachel said quietly, "with glitter in it, or something. Looks like she's glowing. Do you think it would be weird to ask her where she got it?"

"Maybe wait until her second day in school," replied Grace, "before you ask what's in her bathroom cabinet."

Rachel wrinkled her nose and scowled softly.

"Mr. Collins is smiling so wide, it looks like his head might fall off." Adie giggled.

"He's probably racking his brains to try and guess what brand of moisturizer she uses," said Grace, turning to wink at Rachel, who stuck out her tongue in reply.

"Anything you need," beamed Mr. Collins, "I'm just down the hallway."

"You're *very* kind, Mr. Collins." Ms. Gold's voice was like honey. "I think I will manage just fine." She turned to face the class. "And I'm looking forward to getting to know my new class. Shall we start?"

Mr. Collins seemed disappointed at the polite dismissal but took the hint, waving cheerfully as he left.

Grace had never been a big fan of geography, and Adie and Rachel liked it even less, but there was something about the way Ms. Gold explained things that made the world come to life around them. They could almost smell the spices in the air of Mumbai and hear the great crashing water of Niagara Falls. The entire class hung on her every word, raising their hands enthusiastically when asked a question and arguing over who got to scrawl the answer on the whiteboard.

"I can't really explain it," Adie said in the lunchroom later, trying to avoid watching Jenny squish a chocolate bar into her ham sandwich. "It's like all that stuff that Mr. Gains used to talk about is actually *interesting*. Like if you say it the right way, it all sounds really cool."

"We're doing volcanoes next time," said Grace. "And I just can't wait!"

"You two have lost your marbles," Jenny said through a large mouthful of chocolate and ham.

"I thought it was cool too," said Rachel.

"All three of you have lost your marbles," said Una, staring at her friends. "Geography's the worst subject ever."

"That's because you have Ms. Lynch," Rachel replied. "I know for a fact she's had at least four kids fall asleep in her class."

"Speaking of boring classes," said Grace, "we're doing ferns tonight."

Everyone groaned. Ms. Lemon's class was better than Mrs. Quinlan's, but it was still all weeds. Weeds, weeds, and more weeds.

✳ ✳ ✳

"The woods are that way, Miss."

"I thought you girls might need a break from plant life this evening," Ms. Lemon replied. "So today we're going to visit Mr. Pamuk."

"Who's Mr. Pamuk?" said Grace.

"Mr. Pamuk," their teacher replied, "is an invaluable

resource for any witch in this area. He provides the necessary supplies that the woods cannot."

"You mean like the chi orb we used to catch the lost souls in? Stuff like that?"

"Precisely. He has all the paraphernalia any witch could possibly need for any enchantment. Or, at least, he can order it in within five to seven working days. His shop will soon become your new best friend."

Mr. Pamuk's shop turned out to be called The Penny Farthing, a tattered old newsstand near the edge of town. It was the kind of shop that stocked all sorts of colorful, sugary candy and lollipops in massive glass jars. The faded red-brown sign, written in sloping, joined letters above the open door, was barely visible, as was the little painting of the old bicycle that was its namesake. Grace wondered how anyone could have cycled a penny farthing. The bike seat perched on top of a giant front wheel with a tiny back wheel behind. It looked like something out of a circus. *You'd have to be pretty brave to cycle down the street on that contraption*, she thought.

"Not that way, girls," said Ms. Lemon, leading them past the door and down the alleyway beside it. "It's not the newsstand we're interested in."

Stooping to pluck a daisy from a clump of unexpected wildflowers halfway down the potholed alley, she tore the petals between her fingers and scattered the pieces against the shop wall. A heavy perfume suddenly filled the air, and the girls watched, openmouthed, as the old red bricks pulled apart, dropping to the ground, which sank under their weight. The walls folded downward to reveal worn stone steps beneath a brickwork archway.

"Now *that*," Una exclaimed, clasping her hands and hopping up and down, "is more like it!"

"Is that there all the time?" Grace was so delighted she was almost dancing on her tiptoes.

"It's kept well hidden," Ms. Lemon said, "but it's always there."

"Awesome!" Jenny gasped. "Can we go in?"

"You're here to learn, so off you go."

Grace made the first tentative steps down, gripping

Una's hand behind her. The smell of perfume got stronger, catching in her throat as she stepped farther into the darkness. There, at the base of the steps, she could see a faint light, which grew and grew until she reached a large cavern, illuminated by numerous torches along walls that dripped with damp. The room was filled with coffers and tables, draped in dark-colored cloths, and each flat surface was in turn covered with trinkets and figurines. Larger objects lay strewn across the floor or leaned against the weeping stone. The air was thick with the smell of incense, damp rock, and old wood.

"Welcome!" said a man's voice.

2
ms. gold

Mr. Pamuk stood in the center of the room with his arms raised above his smiling face. He looked, for all the world, like he had been waiting there his whole life to greet them.

"What a delight to have new customers! Please come in, come in, look around! All brand-new faces, what a delight! A new generation of witches. May I welcome you most warmly!"

Grace smiled politely as he continued his enthusiastic greetings, his speech light with the soft staccato of an Indian accent.

"Here, an Ursian talisman. These are extremely hard

to come by. And here, a first edition of *Nocturnal Habits of the Indonesian Ogre*. Very rare. Ah," he said, pointing to a small statuette Jenny had plucked from a coffer, "you are more interested in the dark arts, I see."

"No dark arts, Mr. Pamuk." Ms. Lemon ducked her head beneath the stone roof as she entered the cavern. "My girls are fledglings. We'll start with the basics."

"How lovely to see you, Ms. Lemon. You've become a tutor in witchcraft as well as your beloved French?" He raised his hand to his mouth and whispered loud enough for Grace to hear, "Keepers of the demon well?"

"Future keepers of the well, I hope. But we will see."

"In that case," the shopkeeper replied, sweeping his hand in a wide arc, "let the teaching begin!"

Mr. Pamuk shuffled them from table to table, like an enthusiastic tour guide, pointing out the simplest tools of the trade.

"Mortar and pestle, the Wiccan's wooden spoon. So many enchantments require one. A fine sieve, for the draining of crushed leaves and flowers. An antique Medean Oculofero, for the removal of frog's eyes."

"Ugh!" Adie gasped.

"Don't worry." Pamuk chuckled. "There are many synthetic alternatives nowadays. More animal friendly to use and a lot less slippery."

"What's this?" Una picked a long piece of white driftwood from an umbrella basket and held its curling three-pronged claw up to the light.

"A demon hook," the man replied, taking the implement to demonstrate its use. "You swing it underneath, catching the demon beneath the chin, then pull sharply to rip the head from the body."

"Whoa! Gross!"

"And a little impractical. Takes quite a bit of force to remove the head, and a physical fight with a demon is hardly ideal. Not to mention the fact that the poor human under possession is also beheaded. It was used by the ancients but is more a collector's item now."

The tour continued with the more benign items on display, and Grace drifted away from the others, distracted by the shiny, jeweled objects littered across the tables. She gently tapped a silver charm that hung on one corner of a gilded mirror, smiling as a tiny bell inside responded with a long, delicate chime. Her reflection in the mirror smiled back but seemed, somehow, farther away than it should be.

Grace's brow creased as she puzzled over how the glass appeared to have depth, like she could reach inside it and tug her own hair. Her gaze was drawn to the center of the mirror and she noticed a small spiral of mist twist its way from the middle of her reflection outward, until it almost covered the mirror. She felt strangely woozy. The rambling chatter of her friends became muted in the background, and she felt herself being drawn closer and closer to the surface of the glass.

The mist swelled and shrank, revealing the rough shape of a face; she could just make out a pair of eyes, one a deep blue, the other, a strange, opaque white. Grace opened her mouth to say something, and a mouth opened in the mist. She smiled—but the mouth didn't smile back.

Grace raised one hand and reached her fingers

toward the face. Suddenly the mouth stretched impossibly wide and launched itself at her. Screaming, she fell back on the stone floor and scrambled away, kicking at the mirror's gilded frame as she went.

"Grace!" She felt Ms. Lemon grip her arms and help her to her feet. "Are you all right?"

"That mirror tried to eat me!" Grace pointed an accusing finger at the mirror, its surface already back to normal, reflective glass.

"It's all right, my dear," said Mr. Pamuk. "An enchanted looking glass is still just a looking glass."

"But there was something, someone, in it. It jumped out at me!"

"Merely a reflection. Of another person, another creature, maybe in another world. But just a reflection. You're quite safe here."

"Perhaps we've learned enough for today, Mr. Pamuk," said Ms. Lemon, nodding to the girls to remind them of their manners. "Thanks so much for your time."

The girls echoed her thanks, glancing worriedly

at Grace as they climbed the stone steps toward the brickwork archway and out into the alley. Grace heard the scraping of brick against brick as the doorway folded shut behind them.

"Are you sure you're okay?" Ms. Lemon said gently. "Mr. Pamuk's right, you know, you have nothing to fear. Whatever it was wasn't really in the shop. It couldn't hurt you."

"I'm fine, Miss, thanks. Really, I'm okay."

✳✳✳

As the girls walked home, Una kicked sulkily at the grass beneath her feet.

"I wish I'd seen it, whatever it was, in the mirror. Very cool." She scrunched her face in mock horror and clawed her hands dramatically in the air. "The Mirrorman!"

"Knock it off, Una!" Grace replied, slapping at the clawed hands. "And it wasn't cool. It was really scary."

"'Course it was. Sorry, Grace."

"It does sound really scary," Adie said, linking Grace's arm. "I'm relieved it wasn't me who saw it. You're not going to have nightmares, or anything, are you?"

"I'll be fine." Grace couldn't help but smile at her friend's caring nature.

"How good was this trip, though?" said Jenny. "We saw a magic door to a magic shop, and Grace saw a ghost in an enchanted mirror. Finally, something better than weeds!"

Grace had to admit that, even having had a nasty scare, this lesson had been way better than all their witchcraft classes so far. She hoped she'd told Adie the truth, and she wouldn't have nightmares that night. She tried not to think of the misty face in the mirror, with its strange eyes, one staring blue and one clouded white.

In the silence of their geography class, Ms. Gold's amber eyes glowed through the gray smoke spilling from the volcano's open top.

"Stamp your feet on the ground. Does it feel solid?"

A few students tapped their feet hesitantly, looking a little confused.

"Harder. Stamp your feet. Try and make a crack in the floor!"

Some giggling followed as everyone stamped their feet, some gripping the seats of their chairs as they hammered both heels on the ground. Ms. Gold stood up and raised her hands for silence.

"Does it feel solid? Did you crack the floor?"

More giggles as the students replied with mixed yeses and nos.

"Feels solid, doesn't it? But Earth's surface isn't solid at all. Below this thin layer of hard ground, the planet is boiling hot, more than nine thousand degrees Fahrenheit. It's so hot that even rock melts and churns like a pot of oil. And the ground we walk on isn't still either. Every person in the world is walking on a moving plate that floats on that churning molten rock. Hard to imagine, isn't it?"

She waved her hand through the smoke of the

model volcano in front of her desk. "It would be easy to forget what lies in the center of our planet, were it not for these extraordinary reminders. When the pressure beneath the ground builds up too much, it pushes through a weak spot in Earth's crust in an explosion of liquid rock."

She flicked her fingers above the volcano as red and yellow fluid burst from its mouth, spitting into the air in a mini-fireworks display. Grace gasped and leaned forward as the liquid spilled on the sides of the miniature mountain, thickening as it rolled slowly downhill.

"Magma from below the surface," Ms. Gold continued, "becomes lava above ground. Still searing hot, it destroys anything it touches, cooling to solid rock around its victims. In the city of Pompeii, ravaged by the eruption of Mount Vesuvius in 79 CE, the rock that formed was littered with holes, perfect shapes of the poor souls swallowed alive by rolling lava."

"Awesome," said a voice from the back of the class.

Grace was as riveted as everyone else, but couldn't

keep her eyes off the volcano model. How did it work? It wasn't some papier-mâché mound filled with corn syrup, like the sort of thing you'd usually see in school. It billowed smoke. It spat out lava that thickened and hardened to look like rock. It was so…so real.

"So, imagine"—Ms. Gold's voice lowered almost to a whisper—"the last moments of those doomed citizens of Pompeii as they were consumed by their own planet. And never forget that your home is a fiery ball of molten rock."

***

"Do you think we could switch classes, if we asked?" sighed Jenny in the D block hallway. "Ms. Lynch talked for forty minutes straight about oxbow lakes today. Her voice is so monotonous, it's like listening to a food mixer on low."

"You should ask," Rachel replied. "I actually look forward to geography now, it's so cool."

"Those poor people in Pompeii," said Adie. "Do

you know what happened there? There was this volcano—"

"And they all died," Jenny interrupted. "Yeah, we read about it in history last year."

"They didn't just die," Adie said, her face crumpled like it had happened only yesterday. "They were covered in lava. They choked to death on poisonous gases before they burned away to nothing. And all that was left of them were these empty spaces in the rock where their bodies used to be. It's so horrible."

"Where did she get that volcano, do you think?" asked Grace. "I mean, did you see it work? It was like the real thing."

"Yeah," said Rachel. "That was awesome. It spewed out lava and everything."

"She didn't make that herself—there's no way. Where do you think she got it?"

"Bought it online or something. You can get models of anything nowadays."

"But it was so real."

"Well, if you're going to ask her where she got it,

would you mind asking her about her foundation as well? Still can't figure out what it is. I tried all the brands in the drugstore on Saturday, and none of them glowed like that."

"Watch it," Jenny said suddenly. "The Beast looks like she is on the warpath."

Grace followed Jenny's gaze to the beefy mass in the corner of the A block. Tracy Murphy, also known as "the Beast," had an unfortunate seventh grader less than half her size pinned against the wall. Her dark eyes, heavily lined with blue eyeliner, were made all the more menacing by the severe slicked-back pony-tail that held her dark red curls, pulling the skin of her cheeks and forehead back in an unnatural leer.

"Well, I don't see any lunch in your bag," Tracy growled.

"There's no lunch in your bag," one of her loyal henchmen, Bev, echoed. She leaned against a door-way, shaking out the last few items from the girl's backpack on the floor. Snickering, she dropped the backpack and pushed a small comb through the front of the enormous beehive hairdo that perched on top of her head. Trish, the other half of Tracy's devoted posse, pulled a comb from her pocket and mirrored her friend's actions, frowning as the comb got stuck.

"So that means you have lunch money," said the Beast, "and I want it."

The girl shook her head, struggling to breathe.

"I don't have any money, I swear."

"Leave her alone!"

Grace jumped as Jenny's voice boomed across the room. She just managed to stop herself from ducking behind her friend, out of the Beast's eyeline.

"I said, leave her alone," Jenny repeated.

The tiny seventh grader slid down the wall, touching her toes to the ground, as Tracy turned to face Grace and her friends.

"Oh yeah?" sneered the Beast. "Or what, friend of the Freak?"

"Or what?" repeated Bev.

"Friend of the Freak," Trish followed, looking a little uncertain as she tugged at the small comb still trapped in her hair. Grace wondered if she was expected to join in.

"I'm not going to do anything," said Jenny. "But I can't speak for Una."

Grace glanced at Una, who hadn't stepped forward but made a nervous attempt at a threatening look that came out more like a goofy smile. The previous year, Una had been briefly possessed by a demon, and had had a truly savage appearance. Jenny was obviously hoping this memory was still fresh in Tracy's mind. Not to mention the brutal punch that the possessed non-Una had given Tracy, which had caused a giant welt on one cheek and got her suspended from school.

"That girl asked to eat at our lunch table today," Jenny lied, "and Una said it was okay."

The Beast snorted, but loosened her grip on the girl's collar.

"Whatever," she replied. "You freaks should stick together anyway."

Tracy walked past the girls, knocking Jenny's shoulder.

"Stick together," said Bev, following her leader.

"Freaks," Trish said, still holding the tangled comb on one side of her head.

"Thanks for that," Una blurted out when they were gone. "What if she'd wanted a fight? I could have been done there."

"Didn't you see her face?" Jenny replied. "She's still scared of you."

"Yeah? For how long, though?"

"Are you okay?" Grace asked the seventh grader, stooping to help her pick up her belongings that lay strewn across the floor.

"Yes, thanks," the girl said in a tiny voice. "Thank you."

"No problem," said Jenny. "You want to eat lunch at our table today, just in case?"

The girl swept her long, black hair from her face, revealing large, brown puppy-dog eyes, and smiled.

"Yes. If that would be all right."

The six girls soon found a table in their lunchroom large enough for all of them.

"Don't you have anything for lunch, um, sorry, what's your name?" Grace asked, sitting down.

"Delilah," the girl replied, shyly pulling a chair out.

"I'm Grace. This is Jenny, Adie, and Rachel. And the scary one over there is Una."

"Very funny," said Una, with her mouth full. "I'd have looked scarier if you'd given me a heads-up on the plan."

Jenny giggled and pulled a Snickers bar from her pocket. Grace looked expectantly at Delilah and waved her tinfoiled sandwich to remind her of the question.

"Oh, um, my mother forgot to get stuff for lunch today," the girl replied.

"Didn't she give you some money to get something?"

"She forgot, I forgot. She meant to give me some, but she forgot."

"I don't mind sharing with you," said Jenny, holding out her lunch box.

"No!" the others cried in chorus, for Jenny had the unfortunate habit of ruining perfectly good sandwiches by putting chocolate bars and other candy in them.

"I'd take the Snickers out of her half," Jenny grumbled.

"Here," said Rachel, holding out her sandwiches, "you can have half of mine. I don't like salami anyway because it gives me the worst pimples."

Delilah smiled gratefully and took one.

"I like your accent," Adie said, smiling. "Where's it from?"

"My family's Romani," said Delilah. "We just moved here. Me and my mom, I mean."

"You're Italian?" said Una.

"No, Romani. My family travels around a lot, but mostly we lived in Moldova. My uncle has a farm there, and my grandmother prefers it there."

"You travel with your whole family?"

"With some of my uncles and aunts, yes. And cousins."

"Sounds nice," said Adie.

"It was. I miss it a lot."

"How come you're here?"

"My mother wanted to come here. She and my grandmother don't really... She doesn't like Moldova."

"What about your dad?"

Delilah's olive skin flushed a little.

"I…I don't know where he is."

"Oh, I'm sorry." Adie frowned.

There was an awkward moment of silence until Grace said, "Well, you're welcome to hang out with us whenever you want. Especially if the Beast keeps giving you grief."

Delilah's brow furrowed.

"Beast?"

"What we call Tracy Murphy," said Jenny through her chocolate sandwich, "because she's, you know, a beast."

3
the old coven

"What does it look like again?" said Grace, gazing up into the leafy canopy of the woods.

"Oval leaf, dark green, blah, blah, blah."

Grace sighed and pulled the weathered sheet of paper from Jenny's hands.

"We're not going to win our glitter pens if you're not even going to try."

"I've got all the glitter pens I need, thanks," replied Jenny. "Plus, we might as well let Una win. You know how she gets when she loses."

"It's not just about winning. We should be learning this stuff. Getting good at it."

"You're good at memorizing things. Why don't you just learn all this stuff, and whenever we need to collect a plant for a spell or something, we'll just ask you."

"So I do all the work. Thanks a lot."

"You're welcome. Hey, what's that?"

Jenny reached up and tapped a leaf on a low-lying branch. A small butterfly flitted from the leaf, its golden wings catching the last of the evening sun in tiny bursts of light.

"Whoa! I've never seen one that color before! It's amazing. It looks like it's made of gold."

"Look," said Grace, pointing to their right, "there's another one."

As they watched, a third, then a fourth tiny butterfly fluttered upward, wings glittering like little gems. The girls followed the insects, mesmerized by their prettiness, occasionally pretending to catch them, which caused the little creatures to flicker their precious wings even faster and the girls to giggle with delight. They followed them to a clearing in the forest and then stopped, openmouthed, at the sight before them. Thousands upon thousands of golden butter-flies danced as far as they could see. They covered the forest floor, smothered rocks and small bushes, and filled the branches of every tree. Grace had to squint against the light as her eyes adjusted to the world of gold around her.

"Oh my God!" said Jenny. "It's so beautiful!"

"I see you've caught me," a soft voice said. Grace dropped her gaze, and there, in the middle of the clearing, with a basket of weeds hanging on one arm, stood Ms. Gold.

"Come over here," the woman said. "They won't get under your feet, I promise."

The girls inched their way forward and, sure enough, a path appeared among the gold to make way. The rising butterflies swarmed around them; Grace felt like she was in a snow globe filled with glitter.

"They keep me company," said Ms. Gold, "when I'm collecting. The woods can be so dull, sometimes, don't you think?"

"What are they?" breathed Grace. "Where did they come from?"

The teacher gave her a sympathetic smile.

"I'm not sure I should tell you. It's supposed to be a secret."

"Are you…I mean, are you—"

"What the heck?" Una appeared at the other end of the clearing, with Adie close behind her. "Rachel, come here and look at this. There're gold…butterflies. They're butterflies! Golden butterflies everywhere!"

"Hey, Una," called Rachel's voice from farther back in the woods. "Stop trying to distract me! Just because you're losing again!"

"No, seriously. Come here and look at this. It's… it's magic."

Rachel stumbled into Adie and Una, and froze.

"How…what… Wait a minute, is that Ms. Gold?"

"Hello, girls," Ms. Gold said, smiling. "Come over here and join your friends. The insects are perfectly harmless, and you can appreciate the full effect much better from here."

Rachel wandered forward, gazing around her as she went and grinning at the sparkling motion-filled air. Adie kept hold of the back of Una's sweater as they joined the others, looking amazed but a little frightened.

"Where did they come from?" she asked. "Why are there so many?"

"I suppose I can be a little overenthusiastic," said Ms. Gold.

"Did you make them?" said Grace, lowering her voice to a whisper. "Are they magic?"

Ms. Gold just smiled again, raising her hand and allowing a tiny butterfly to settle on her outstretched fingers.

"I knew it," said Grace. "I knew that volcano was real. I just knew it!"

"Anything to help my students learn," her teacher replied. "The world is filled with wonder, and I don't want them to miss out on any of it."

"You're a witch!" Adie gasped.

Ms. Gold blew gently on her fingertips and watched the shimmering butterfly fly away.

"And I'm not the only one collecting herbs this evening." She nodded to the small bag of leaves on Adie's arm.

"We're witches too, Ms. Gold!" Una said excitedly.

"We're not really," Grace said quickly. "We're kind of… We're just learning."

"I knew there was something special about you girls!" Ms. Gold replied. "Five witches working together. You must cast the most tremendous spells."

"We did a while ago," said Jenny. "We did all these spells, but they didn't quite work out and—"

"We don't do spells," Grace interrupted loudly, giving Jenny a look. "I mean, we did try a few before, but they didn't work out well. We're learning magic properly now, so we don't do spells."

"You don't cast spells?" Ms. Gold looked puzzled. "Witches that don't cast spells, how strange. How do you learn if you don't cast spells?"

"We're learning all about herbs and things, stuff for making potions. When we know all the theory, we'll be able to do magic safely."

"That sounds like a peculiar way to teach aspiring witches. Who is tutoring you?"

Right on cue, they heard Ms. Lemon's voice from the woods.

"Girls? Where have you gone?" she called. "None of you will beat the time at this rate."

She stepped into the clearing and paused, astonished, as she took in the dazzling swarm of tiny golden creatures. Her gaze then landed on Ms. Gold. All the color drained from her face.

"Beth?" Ms. Gold stepped forward and smiled widely. "Beth, is it really you? Oh, I have been dying to see you for so long! How strange to be back here—the two of us!"

Ms. Lemon didn't move a muscle but gasped one word.

"Meredith."

"Meredith?" Grace whispered as Ms. Gold made her way toward their frozen French teacher. "Wasn't she the other girl in their coven?"

"Yeah," Jenny replied. "They had a big fight or

something. But she disappeared, didn't she? Left when they finished school."

"Well, she's obviously back."

"Yeah. Isn't it great?"

"I don't know."

"What do you mean?" Rachel asked Grace.

"What did they fight over?" said Grace. "I mean, are they still friends?"

"Not judging from the look on Ms. Lemon's face," said Adie.

"They were just kids back then. I'm sure they'll work it out," Una said. Her face brightened. "Ooh! Maybe we can get Ms. Gold to give us lessons as well."

"That would be awesome," said Jenny. "I bet she'd let us do some spells. Come on, let's go ask."

As the girls approached the two women, Ms. Lemon was looking a little less shocked, but not any friendlier.

"Miss?" Grace said expectantly.

"Come on, girls," Ms. Lemon said abruptly. "We're going."

44

"Don't be that way, Beth," said Ms. Gold, reaching to take her hand, but missing, as it was pulled away. "Can't we let bygones be bygones? Things are so different now. And I understand you're tutoring these girls. With Vera, is it? I'd be happy to help. It's so important to train the next generation, but it is a lot of work. I'll share the burden."

"We don't need your help, thank you. Vera and I are doing just fine."

"Teaching them to identify elements, but not showing them how to use them? Is that just fine?"

"We're teaching them about responsibility, Meredith, something you could never understand."

"You're still so afraid, Beth. And you'll just teach them to be afraid. You're not teaching witches, you're teaching normal people to use witchcraft. It's nothing more than dabbling. A true witch has magic in her soul. It's a part of her, not just something she uses."

"Girls," Ms. Lemon said sharply, "I said we're leaving. It's getting late."

"Witches don't have to fear the dark," said Ms. Gold

softly. "You would know that, Beth, if you would just fully embrace what you are."

"Girls! Come on!"

Ms. Lemon didn't wait for them but marched off, and they didn't lag behind. Grace glanced back at Ms. Gold, who smiled sadly at her, the shimmering gold around her popping into blackness as the butterflies disappeared. Nobody dared ask Ms. Lemon what had just happened. Instead they stumbled on in the growing darkness, struggling to keep up with her furious stride. When they reached open ground near the school parking lot, Ms. Lemon turned to face them.

"She's teaching at the school?"

"She's our new geography teacher, Miss," replied Grace. "Haven't you seen her there?"

"No," Ms. Lemon said sharply. "She's obviously been avoiding me until now."

The French teacher sighed and stared into the distance for a moment.

"Is something wrong, Miss? Did we do something?"

"No, my dear girls, you did nothing wrong."

"Maybe Ms. Gold could help out, Miss," Jenny said quietly. "Give us extra lessons."

Ms. Lemon looked a little hurt before her face hardened.

"Vera and I will teach you everything you need to know. I want you to keep your distance from Ms. Gold. Is that clear?"

"But she's our teacher, Miss."

"Outside of class. Is that clear?"

She raised one eyebrow and kept it up until she received a reluctant chorus of "Yes, Miss."

"Good. Now let's all go home."

✳✳✳

"Mrs. Quinlan," Jenny said bravely during their lesson the next day, "we met the other girl from your coven, Ms. Gold. She's a teacher at school now."

"So I've heard," the woman replied with her back to them as she scrawled squeakily on her old kitchen blackboard.

"She offered to help teach us, but Ms. Lemon thinks it's a bad idea."

Mrs. Quinlan kept writing and didn't reply.

Grace glared at her friend, willing her not to push it any further, but Una was giving Jenny an enthusiastic thumbs-up.

"What do you think?" Jenny asked.

"I think," said the woman, dropping her chalk and turning to face them, "that you have two witches teaching you, free of charge, and that's enough."

"Ms. Gold says we should be doing spells while we learn. That that's how we should be learning."

"Is that so?"

Jenny gulped and kept going. "I wouldn't mind having another teacher. You know, just to have another viewpoint. Another way of looking at things. I think it's a good idea."

"Do you?" The pale eyes were becoming alarmingly hooded. "And what about the rest of you?"

She turned her stare on the others, who all tried to look at anything in the room but Mrs. Quinlan. Grace picked at the table with her fingernail, Rachel cleared her throat uncomfortably, Una bit her lip, and Adie give a noncommittal whimper. Jenny exhaled noisily at the betrayal.

"I think Beth and I have been too soft on you, that's what it is," said the woman, stroking the ears of a cat on the table. "You're all spoiled rotten. You know what you need? Some good honest labor."

Grace exchanged worried looks with the others.

"I have a list of items here that are essential tools for any witch. I've got them all, of course, in the house. The attic, to be precise. Been a while since I've used most of them. Might take some digging around to find them."

The woman's chapped lips widened to reveal her yellowed teeth.

"Off you go."

Grace felt queasy at the thought of rummaging around in Mrs. Quinlan's attic. God knows what was up there. And if the state of her house was anything to go by, they could be up there for days. The girls didn't protest for fear of worse punishment, but the pain was written all over their faces. They picked their way through the meowing cats that lay scattered throughout the kitchen and hall, and made their way upstairs. At the top they could see a square hole in the ceiling above a very decrepit-looking ladder. The ladder wobbled worryingly, squeaking a little, as each of them mounted it and climbed carefully into the dark room. Grace brought up the rear, following Jenny's feet into the gloom and coughing uncontrollably as dust filled her lungs.

"Where's the light?"

She heard a dull thump and a groaning "Ow!" from Jenny before the room gently illuminated. Jenny frowned at the filthy light switch and wiped her finger on her sweater.

"This is, by far, the worst day of my whole entire life," Una grumbled.

"That's a bit of an exaggeration, Una." Grace stepped into the maze of dusty boxes, hissing as her leg glanced painfully off the jagged edge of an old trunk.

"This is going to take all night!"

"Couldn't we just say, 'We're not doing it'?" said Rachel. "I mean, we're not in school. This is slave labor."

"I guess we could," Grace replied. "But I think she'd kick us out for good."

"And she'd probably curse us," Adie said, widening her eyes as Grace shook her head. "I wouldn't put it past her!"

"Let's just get on with it," said Jenny. "The sooner we start, the sooner it's over."

The girls worked solidly for two hours and got more than halfway through the list. By then, they were covered with dust and dirt and Rachel was nursing a broken nail. Una lay sprawled across several piles of boxes shouting instructions at the others.

"No," she said, turning the list in her hand and examining the crudely drawn diagram. "You're looking for a Y-shape, like a slingshot. That's not a Y-shape, Grace. Try again."

"Would you like to come here and do some actual work, Una?" said Grace.

"No thanks, not really."

Jenny snorted and threw an old blanket at her. Una squealed, swatting at the moth-eaten wool and rolling onto the floor, taking one of the dusty boxes with her. The lid flipped off, spilling the contents everywhere.

"Una!" cried Grace.

"That was Jenny's fault."

"Like we don't have enough to do!"

Grace righted the box and kneeled down to pile the books and wooden ornaments back in.

"Hey, look at this." She wiped the cover of one slim volume with her sleeve and held it up. "Saint John's Yearbook, 1977."

"No way!" Jenny swiped the book and flipped through the pages.

"Do you think Mrs. Quinlan's in there?" said Una.

"Yeah, why else would she have it? Just wondering if we will recognize her." Jenny stopped and jammed her finger into one page. "Look at that. Ms. Bethany Lemon. That's her, leaning against the school gates."

"And that must be Ms. Gold," said Rachel. "Wow, she's barely changed at all. How weird is that?"

"Then that," said Grace, planting her finger on the girl standing between them, "is Mrs. Vera Quinlan—or whatever her last name was back then."

Slouching, with one elbow on the iron gate, the youthful Mrs. Quinlan was the very picture of a 1970s punk: a faded denim jacket over her rumpled school sweater, torn tights, kneesocks pushed to her ankles, and short asymmetric hair spiked into sharp points and certainly dyed (though it was difficult to tell what color in the black-and-white photo). Her eyes were heavily lined in black, and the glint of several piercings poked through the spiky hairdo.

"Hold. The. Phone," said Una, pushing her face right up to the page. "This is so freaky. I'm having an out-of-body experience."

"Vera Miller, she was, before she was Quinlan," Rachel read. "And look at the stuff other kids have written."

Beneath the photo were the obligatory scribbles of other students, written at the end of the school year.

Grace took the book, turning it this way and that as she read.

Take it to the Max, V. You're awesome!!

Diggin' your tunes, V-girl! Keep in touch!

Movin' on and movin' up in the world. Far out V xx

YOU ARE DYN-O-MITE!!

To the grooviest groovy chick I ever met—life won't be the same without you!

The girls looked at each other in surprise.

"Mrs. Quinlan was...popular," said Grace.

"There's friendly stuff scribbled all over this page," said Jenny, "and the next one. Lots of people. Wow."

"And she looked cool," Rachel said. "I mean, actually cool. Look at her hair. My mom went crazy when Una put a few highlights in mine, and you could barely see them."

Grace smiled and ran her fingers over the old, fading photograph.

"They look like they were good friends, don't they?" she said. "Wonder what happened."

***

A soft breeze blew through a kitchen window onto seventeen-year-old Bethany Lemon, who sat at the table, staring into her slightly undercooked oatmeal and tugging at her bangs. It was the summer of 1977, and the yearbook photos were being taken today. She pulled her heavy bangs across one eye, low enough to almost cover her nose, and wondered if she could cover her face altogether.

The pictures were taken individually now that Beth was a senior. No more hiding behind the boy or girl in front; no more subtly glancing off to one side just as the photo was taken, ensuring her face was barely visible in the printed book.

Stephen McFadden had already snapped one of her, Vera, and Meredith by the school gates. "A candid moment," he called it. He had smiled widely and explained, mainly to Vera, how people's real memories of school were rarely captured on film. "Posed images" eclipsed the reality of their teenage years. He preferred to catch a genuine moment, when the subjects were unaware. *We were unaware, all right,* Beth thought bitterly. She hadn't seen the camera in time to avoid it.

"Are you going to eat your breakfast?"

Her mother barely looked up from her own bowl as she spoke, and Beth nodded mechanically. She picked up her spoon and poked at the gooey mess. Her father sat silently on her other side.

Breakfast and dinner were still a family affair in her house, though she couldn't, for the life of her, understand why. There had been a little more conversation at each meal when her brother still lived at home, but that usually broke down when he made excuses and left the table early. Now he lived with his wife in a big house nearly three hours' drive away. They were expecting a baby too. She couldn't blame him. He was creating a happy family life to replace the one he'd never had. Her parents must have been happy at some point, but not in her living memory. They didn't argue; they didn't fight. They just didn't like each other. And she didn't think either of them was particularly fond of her. But still, twice a day, they sat down together and ate in silence.

Today she counted the minutes until she could politely leave and hurry to school to meet her coven. Meredith and Vera were never quiet—they argued all the time—and with them she felt comfortable. She could take a break from her shyness, and from the cloak of unhappiness that shrouded her home. They were kind of her surrogate family. In some ways, they felt more like her real family.

∗∗∗

"Keep moving, Lemon."

A strong hand gripped her elbow before she rounded the school gates and steered her past them.

"Where are we going?"

Vera's numerous piercings jingled slightly as she whipped her head around, scoping out the area for teachers and other authority figures. When she was satisfied they were in the clear, she smiled at Beth.

"The river."

"They're taking the yearbook photos today."

Vera huffed impatiently. "We'll be back in time for them."

"No rush," said Beth. "What are we doing at the river?"

"Collecting. We're going to see the Old Wagon today."

"I wish you wouldn't call her that."

Vera's arm remained tucked into Beth's as they hurried past the woods along the quiet road that led to the river.

"What should I call her then?"

"How about 'Mrs. Allan,'" replied Beth. "That's her name."

"Old Wagon suits her just fine."

"Vera, she's…elderly! You should be nice."

"Just 'cause the woman's so old and decrepit that she can't leave her house, does that mean I'm required to undergo a complete personality transplant? You're just soft."

"If I were in her position, I'd want people to be kind and nice to me."

"Well, you're not. So thank your lucky stars."

The sound of rushing water grew louder as they walked on, and soon the river was in sight. Carefully, they slid down the bank to where Meredith stood waiting.

"Mostly aquatic stuff she wants today," she said. "Spawning brook lamprey, if you can find them."

"What does she want with brook lamprey?" Vera sniffed.

"Spawning ones only," replied Meredith. "She preserves them in vinegar. They're good for perception-altering spells. Says she can take a vacation to Spain… in her mind."

"Hmph." Vera looked ready to make a snide comment, when Beth noticed her features suddenly brighten. "That would be a Four Poles spell, wouldn't it?"

"You can do it that way," said Meredith. "But she could manage it by herself. It's possible."

"But it's better with four people."

"Yeah, it's better with four."

Vera hunkered down on the bank, apparently digging for lamprey.

"Much better," she said. "Better than one, two, or even three."

Meredith's face kept its usual coolness, but Beth's heart suddenly thumped in her chest. Four witches were better than three? What was Vera saying? They had been three for years—it was a great Wiccan number, Vera had said so herself. Why would they want a fourth? Beth watched as Vera calmly picked through the mud, wondering how her friend could suggest something so drastic. Panic was already breaking out a sweat across Beth's brow, and she looked to Meredith to put an immediate end to the idea. But the blond girl simply stared, then turned and began searching in the shallow water. Beth didn't want change. The coven was her family, her only security, and she didn't want anything to break that.

An unfamiliar feeling rushed through her—anger at Vera's callousness. She was aware that she was the weak one, that she needed the other two more than they needed her. But until this moment, she didn't believe it really mattered. They were sisters and would always do right by each other. But now Vera was bored. Bored with her and with the coven. Gray clouds settled over the sun, dulling the reflections of the river and turning the water to a silty brown. The other two carried on as usual, but Beth knew, with that one little sentence, everything had changed.

Mrs. Allan's wheezing breath whistled in time to the ticking of the old cuckoo clock on the wall. She was a large woman, squeezed into a flimsy armchair that had fraying beige upholstery and shiny mahogany legs. Her upper body tilted forward slightly, as if she was perpetually on the point of getting up. But she never did. Her ancient lungs and weak heart kept her confined to her room and, for the most part, to her chair. Her eyelids had the unnerving habit of drifting shut when she was still wide awake, though it seemed the woman could see right through them. She reveled in startling her young visitors with sharp outbursts, chastising them for touching some ornament or other without permission when she had appeared to be in a deep sleep.

"A couple of lamprey, as promised." Meredith placed a jar on the side table in front of Mrs. Allan.

"Spawning?" the woman growled.

"Of course."

"And another," said Vera, banging a second jar on the table, "'cause we're so generous."

The woman's half-closed eyes watched Vera without expression. Then suddenly she shrieked, "Tea!"

She lifted her heavy foot and stamped twice on the floor.

"Tea!" she yelled again.

There was the sound of clattering dishes from the room below and, within minutes, a gaunt woman, with a tight bun of gray hair, flitted into the room and deposited a tray on the little table. Beth shot her a quick smile, but the woman scurried out of the room, head bowed, without responding.

"Tea," Mrs. Allan said, quietly this time, and Meredith poured out four cups. This was a familiar ritual. They were never offered milk or sugar, and Beth found it hard to stomach the bitter, black liquid. But the old woman's temper flared up if any of them refused to finish an entire cup. When all were empty, she would pick up each in turn and stare into the swollen, soaked leaves in the bottom of the cup. She could do this for ages—sometimes as long as an hour—and the three girls would have to sit silently the whole time.

It gave Beth the willies to watch the old woman twist a delicate teacup in her hand, staring intently into the bottom, a smile occasionally playing on her lips. And she suspected their visits to Mrs. Allan were more about those tea leaves than the trade of flora and fauna for items the girls couldn't get on their own.

"We want a scrying bowl," Vera said, before Mrs. Allan had placed the final cup back on the table. "In good condition, no garbage."

The old woman tapped one long, pointed fingernail on the edge of the teacup. There was a faint ringing, scraping sound, as the fingernail was dragged up and down the delicate porcelain.

"If you had one to spare," Meredith said, as if Vera had never spoken, "we would very much appreciate a scrying bowl, Mrs. Allan. Our skills are progressing. We could never hope to master the reading of leaves, but the simpler task of scrying might be in our reach."

The woman tilted her head to look up at Meredith with sleepy, malicious eyes.

"The cabinet on the right," she said. "The olive green one. Don't touch the red."

"You're very kind."

"It's a trinket," the woman replied, regarding Meredith steadily. "Nothing compared to, say, a crystal ball."

Beth glanced at Meredith as if to say, *What did she mean by that?* But Meredith was hurriedly snatching the bowl from the cabinet and wrapping it in a scarf.

"We'll leave you be," she said, buckling her schoolbag.

"Return anytime." The woman was smirking like Beth had never seen before. "There's always tea."

✳✳✳

"What was she rambling on about crystal balls for?" said Vera, as the three girls made their way from North Street toward the school.

"I think her mind is failing a bit," replied Meredith. "She's starting to wander."

"Yeah, no kidding. She's read our leaves a dozen times, and still…every single time. I'd swear it's the only time she looks vaguely happy. What's so entertaining?"

"I guess there must be something eventful in our future that's worth watching," said Beth. "Maybe we really make it as witches. Maybe she's watching our success."

"Not likely," said Vera. "There's something twisted in that old trout. She'd get more joy from watching a train wreck."

"We're late for the yearbook photos," Meredith said quickly. "Come on."

Beth groaned as they picked up the pace.

4
a little glamour

Grace tossed the few notebooks that had fallen out of her locker back in, sneaking a glance at the old 1977 year-book that sat tucked in on one side. She took a quick look over her shoulder, then pulled the book out and flicked through the dog-eared pages to the photo of Vera Quinlan and the others. The seventeen-year-old Vera looked how every cool kid in school looks—bored with the world and everything in it. Beth Lemon looked a little shy, with her head bowed and glancing up at the camera with a bashful smile. Meredith Gold, on the other hand, stared right through the lens, her light eyes intense and her expression severe. She didn't have the same glamorous appearance that she had now, but her fair hair and white skin were unmistakable.

"Wow, is that from our school?" a voice said behind her. "The uniform looks kind of the same, but sort of old."

Grace instinctively snapped the book shut and stuck it under her arm. She started to say something evasive, but James O'Connor's smile made the words stick in her throat. She begged her cheeks not to blush. Too late.

"Sorry, didn't mean to be nosy," he said.

"Oh, it's fine," she replied, half pulling the year-book out to show him. "It *is* from our school, from the seventies."

"Wow. Where'd you get it? Can I take a look?"

She ignored his first question and let him flick through the pages.

"It's like looking through a wormhole, or something." He laughed. "It's so weird. Look, there's the back of the school, before the P block was built. It's just a field!"

"Yeah," Grace replied, frantically searching for something else to say. "And take a look at the gym clothes back then. They're so horrible!"

"Aw, no way! Those shorts! That's just wrong."

Grace grinned. Aside from the time she cast a love spell on him (and that didn't really count), this was the longest conversation she'd ever had with James. The realization made the blush spread to her forehead and neck. She gulped, hoping he didn't notice that she was lit up like a Christmas tree. She scratched her jawline, pulling her hair over her cheek in the hope of covering the worst of the redness.

"That's awesome," he said, handing the book back. "I'd better go. Mr. O'Dwyer goes crazy when we're late for PE."

"Okay, bye."

"See you, Grace."

He shot her a polite smile as he left and…was that a little color in his cheeks too? Grace frowned for a second, then shook her head, smiling. She pushed the yearbook into her bag and snapped the locker door shut.

✳✳✳

"They've got her again." Jenny pointed as she and Grace made their way to class. "That little girl. Delilah."

Trish was going through the girl's backpack as Bev looked on, blowing loud-snapping bubbles with her gum. Tracy had Delilah by one shoulder, keeping her in a stooped position, waiting for something inter-esting to pop out of the stolen bag. Grace followed Jenny's determined stride closely, but kept a little behind her friend. With only the two of them, and no Una to freak the Beast out, she felt outnumbered.

"Let go of her!" Jenny didn't waste any time. "And give her back her bag."

Tracy snickered.

"Hey, where's the Freak, friend of the Freak?"

"Yeah, friend of the Freak," said Bev through her gum.

"She'll be here any minute," Grace replied.

"It doesn't matter where Una is," Jenny said very loudly. "Because *I'm* telling you to let her go."

Tracy flicked back her dark red ponytail and raised one hand mockingly to her ear.

"What did you say? Pull her hair out? Okay."

She grabbed a handful of Delilah's black hair and gave it a violent tug. The girl yelped in pain.

"Stop it!" shouted Jenny.

"Give her a kick? All right."

A vicious swift kick to the shins, and Delilah fell to the ground crying.

"Leave her alone!"

"Make her kiss the ground I walk on? If you say so."

Still holding the girl by the scruff of one shoulder, the Beast dunked her head until her forehead hit the ground. Delilah's muffled cries could just be heard over the sniggering of the two henchmen.

"*Stop it!*" Jenny's voice was shrill as she swung her backpack off her shoulder in a wide arc over her head, firing it at Tracy's face. The Beast ducked just in time, letting the bag fly past her, smash through one of the glass panes lining the hallway, and land on the grass outside. There was a stunned silence.

"What's going on down there?" a voice thundered from the main hall.

Tracy let go of Delilah's sweater and made her escape with her two friends in tow, knocking over Grace as she went. Jenny struggled to get Grace and Delilah to their feet at the same time, just as Ms. Gold arrived.

"I heard a crash. What happened?" She glanced at the broken window. "Oh. Does that bag belong to one of you?"

"It wasn't Jenny's fault, Miss," Grace explained. "Tracy Murphy was beating up this girl, and Jenny was just trying to stop her. It was an accident."

"And that's your bag, Jenny?"

Jenny nodded solemnly, putting one arm around a still tearful Delilah.

"She's just a seventh grader," Grace went on, "and she just moved here, Miss. Tracy's been picking on her."

Ms. Gold looked for a long moment at the small girl, but Delilah avoided her gaze.

"What was that?" They heard Mr. Collins's voice coming toward them. "I heard something smash."

Grace felt sick to her stomach as she heard the vice principal approaching. There was no way they weren't going to get in trouble for this.

"Did somebody break something? Is anyone hurt?" He was rounding the corner; he'd be upon them any second.

Grace heard a gentle tinkle of glass and, just as he arrived, she turned to see the window fully restored, gleaming and unbroken, with Jenny's bag still lying on the grass outside. Her mouth dropped open.

"Nothing broken, Mr. Collins, luckily," said Ms. Gold. "These girls were in too much of a hurry and one of them banged into the window, but no injuries and no harm done."

"Oh," said Mr. Collins, inspecting the glass, "I could have sworn I heard something break."

"Cup of tea in the staff room?" Ms. Gold smiled.

The vice principal's face lit up immediately.

"You know, I was just thinking I'd love a cup of tea

right now. Wonderful. Oh, and, uh, be careful, girls, won't you?"

"Lead the way, Mr. Collins," said Ms. Gold, turning to give Grace a wink as she followed the vice principal back down the hallway.

"Did you see that?" Jenny gasped.

"That was *amazing*!" Grace replied.

"Thank God she was here, or I'd have been suspended for sure."

Grace turned to Delilah. "Are you okay?"

She pulled a clean tissue from her pocket and gave it to Delilah, who wiped away the last of her tears.

"Yes," she sniffled. "Thank you."

"Come on," said Jenny, giving her shoulders a squeeze. "Come and have lunch with us."

✳✳✳

Adie and Rachel were watching Ms. Gold like she was the Second Coming. Holding two large bottles, fused together at the neck with one on top of the other, their teacher was demonstrating her "homemade" tornado. One bottle was half-filled with pale green liquid and, when shaken and upturned, the colored water slowly emptied into the bottom bottle, forming a perfect twister in the glass neck. Grace gazed into the spinning vortex. She had seen one of these before—they were all over YouTube—and she wondered where the magic was. Unconsciously, she played the witch's theme from *The Wizard of Oz* in her mind, catching sight of tiny debris in the bottle. She concentrated on the edge of the twister, suddenly picking out a teeny, tiny house spinning in the liquid. She looked closer and could make out miniature figures, cars, and even farm animals caught in the mini-storm. She glanced up at Ms. Gold, who smiled at her knowingly. Her two friends had also spotted the magical extras and were whispering excitedly to one another. Nobody else in the class seemed to notice.

When the bell rang, the three girls stayed in their seats. They waited until everyone else had left in a bustle of chatter and noisy furniture, then sat in silence.

"Time to go home, girls," the teacher said.

Grace didn't answer. She stared at her hands on the table.

"Girls," Ms. Gold said again. "It's time to go home."

"Do we have to, Miss?"

Ms. Gold sighed and sat on the edge of her desk.

"Are you worried about that window?" she asked. "I promise I won't tell anyone."

"It's not that, Miss," Grace replied, still staring at her fingernails. "It's just that…we were wondering if you could…"

"Couldn't *you* teach us, Miss?" Rachel interrupted. "Magic, I mean."

"Beth and Vera are tutoring you," Ms. Gold said, "and they want to keep it that way. I would love to help, I really would. But they'd never allow it."

"We wouldn't have to tell them, Miss. We could keep it a secret."

"I'm not sure that's a good idea."

"Please, Miss," Adie said gently.

The woman sighed again and stared into space for

a moment. Grace gazed pleadingly at her when she looked at them again.

"Small things," Ms. Gold said quickly. "Just a few small, harmless bits and pieces. The big stuff I'll leave to them. Agreed?"

"Yes! Agreed!"

✳✳✳

The following evening, the five girls assembled for their first lesson with Ms. Gold.

"Now where shall we start?" she said, smiling.

All five girls were huddled around one desk, shuffling their feet with excitement.

"Something lovely," said Una. "The golden butterflies!"

"Hmm." Ms. Gold frowned. "That's a little complicated. You need a good grip on your surroundings for that one. How about we start a little smaller. With yourselves."

"With us?"

"The easiest thing to keep control over—yourself. Let's try a little Glamour."

"You mean like making ourselves pretty?" said Rachel. "Yeah!"

"Or ugly, or old, or animallike," said Ms. Gold. "Whatever you want. Glamour is like a sheet between you and the rest of the world, and you can draw whatever you like on it. It doesn't require a potion or anyone else to help. It's just you and your imagination."

"Awesome!"

"Hands out like this." Ms. Gold straightened her arms in front and spread her fingers. "Repeat after me: *Faciem occulta, personam ostende.* Feel that tiny buzz beneath your fingertips? You need to keep hold of that and build it up. Wiggle your fingers."

Una started to flap her hands around.

"*Gently!*" said Ms. Gold. "Gently, at first. Still got it? All right, wiggle a little more now. The buzz should feel stronger; it should be spreading up to your knuckles. Is everyone following me?"

Five heads nodded.

"All right, here comes the difficult part. You want to tip that buzz into your hands and use it before it falls out. So, when you're ready, I want you to take a deep breath, picture *very* clearly in your mind what you want to see in the mirror, scoop your hands up and over your face, keeping your fingers moving all the time—hold on to that buzz—and ripple your hands down without touching your skin. Everyone ready? Then let's go for it. Scoop and ripple down the face!"

Grace's heart was racing as she pictured herself with thick, bouncy locks of curly black hair. However, as she lifted her fingers, she felt the buzzing slip down the sides of her hands and disappear altogether.

"Very good, Rachel!" Ms. Gold exclaimed. "Goodness me, you're a natural Glamourer."

Grace opened her eyes to see Rachel's were a deep shade of purple. Her hair had zipped itself into a stylish bob, and her teeth were blindingly white.

"Mine didn't work right, Miss," Jenny said, leaning over to scrutinize her reflection in the hand mirror in the center of the desk. It looked like she had meant to give herself tiger stripes, but the orange, white, and black had spread across her face in uneven blotches.

"Ah," the teacher replied, "that's lack of clarity in your self-imaging. You imagined the stripes, yes? The colors. But you didn't picture their exact placement on your face. Always remember, girls, Glamour can do wondrous things, but you have to be *specific* about what you want. Otherwise, it dumps the elements in any old order. As you're building the buzz, take a moment to picture *exactly* the result you want. Take your time. There's no rush."

"It didn't work for me at all, Miss," Una said, frowning into the mirror.

"Me neither," said Adie.

"Or me," said Grace.

"There's a knack to catching the buzz," Ms. Gold replied, "so don't despair. Rachel's rather unusual— I've never seen anyone get it perfect on their first go. Just remember the golden rule of witchcraft—"

"Knowledge equals power," said Grace.

Ms. Gold smiled and took Grace's hands, holding her arms out straight.

"Practice makes perfect."

After an hour of Glamouring, Grace still hadn't managed to give herself bouncing black curls, but she had managed to change her eye color from green to blue, and had had an interesting blunder when she tried to make her face like a fish, but made it red-brick instead by glancing out of the window at a wall just as she caught the buzz. They were not outstanding achievements, but she felt wonderfully in control. Even though she didn't always get the result she wanted, the very fact that she could change her appearance made her feel so *witch-like*. Finally, she and the girls were getting somewhere. They weren't just students learning about plants and fungi and all their properties. They were *witches*. Real witches, learning real magic. It was bliss.

"Thanks, Miss, that was so amazing!" chorused the girls, as they prepared to go home.

"Seriously, Miss, that was the best class ever!" Jenny grinned.

"You're very welcome, girls. It's my pleasure."

"Miss?" Una said tentatively.

"Yes, Una."

"What happened to your coven? How come Ms. Lemon and Mrs. Quinlan won't let you teach us?"

Ms. Gold's light-filled eyes darkened as she got up from her chair.

"I don't want to rake up old graves—there's no good in it." She took a deep breath and gave them a big forced smile. "Let's leave the past in the past, shall we?"

5

old spells, like fine wines

Once again, the dense air of Mr. Pamuk's shop was heavy with incense. Grace was wary of being back in the stone cavern and kept a good thirty-foot distance from the enchanted mirror, where she had seen—what? A terrifying face with weird eyes, a creature that had tried to get her.

But Ms. Lemon had insisted they return to the shop for another visit.

"Best to face your fears," she said. "Besides, Mr. Pamuk is a fountain of information. You'll need his advice. Not to mention he's the only decent supplier around here— you can't be a witch without him."

This time the girls were given free rein to wander around the shop as they pleased, picking up items and asking what the more interesting-looking ones were for. Grace thumbed carefully through an ancient spell book. The crunchy brown pages were covered in an indecipherable scrawl of black ink, punctuated with hand-drawn diagrams.

"Do spells go out of date?" she asked. "I mean, we used our ordinary kind of language when we were doing spells. Do the old ones stop working if the language is too old?"

"Not at all," said Mr. Pamuk. "And frequently, like fine wines, spells mature wonderfully with age."

"Do you mean they become stronger?"

"More potent. Yes, very often. The most successful witches will always include some of the oldest spell books in their libraries."

"Mr. Pamuk, this mirror's broken."

Across the room, Una held up a small mirror with a wooden handle. The face of the mirror was shiny, but showed no reflection.

"Careful, Una!" said Grace.

"It's all right, Grace," said Ms. Lemon. "That's a Penzios Mirror, for Reverse Glamour spells—changing the appearance of others."

"Cool!" Una said, smiling into the empty glass. "I'd love to try some *Reverse* Glamour."

"You'd have to master basic Glamour first."

There was a stony silence.

"Yes," Una said robotically. "I would have to learn basic Glamour first."

"What's this?" Jenny rushed in to change the subject. She held up another rather dull-looking ancient book.

"Goodness me," said Mr. Pamuk. "You have a good eye. That's an *Il Fuoco Dormiente*, first edition. One of the finest collections of spells and enchantments ever written. If old spells are fine wines, that's a veritable cellar-full."

Jenny frowned as she lifted the worn cover, running her hand across the aged pages.

"Lovely!" said Grace as she wandered off to another corner of the shop.

One pleasant hour later, and it was time to go. The girls groaned in protest.

Grace lifted a wicker hat off her head, slightly disappointed that Mr. Pamuk couldn't demonstrate its use.

"Unfortunately, it was badly damaged during a fierce battle many centuries ago. Rumor has it, Attila the Hun himself fired an arrow through the artifact, ending its power of invisibility and, sadly, rendering its wearer very visible." Mr. Pamuk smiled fondly as he placed the hat carefully on a wide shelf. "Still, an extraordinary item."

"Jenny," called Ms. Lemon, "I said, it's time to go."

"Coming, Ms. Lemon." With her back to the others, Jenny shuffled with something at a high table before swinging her bag onto her shoulder and turning. "All right. Let's go."

"What were you looking at?" Grace whispered.

"Yeah," said Una. "You missed Grace in a shabby hat *not* going invisible. It was majorly exciting."

Jenny shook her head in warning and hurried up the stone steps.

"Well," said Una, when Ms. Lemon had left them. "You gonna spill?"

Jenny smirked as she rooted in the bottom of her backpack and pulled out a sheet of notebook paper.

"That book I was looking through, with all those spells? Well, I found something really cool."

She unfolded the piece of paper and held it out. Grace leaned in to read Jenny's blue scribbles, but couldn't make any of it out.

"Is that English?"

Jenny tutted. "Yeah. Look, ignore my writing. I'll redo it neatly later. But do you see what it is?"

They all stared and frowned. Jenny tutted again.

"It's a spell for seeing into the past. You can look back into history."

There were a few interested sounds and nodding heads.

"Don't you get it? We can look back and see what happened between Ms. Lemon, Mrs. Quinlan, and Ms. Gold. We can find out what broke up the coven."

"And then we can fix it," said Una. "Genius!"

"Wait, wait, wait," said Grace. "You want to do a spell? We can't. No way. They'd go nuts if they found out."

"Quinlan and Lemon would go nuts," said Jenny. "Ms. Gold wouldn't mind at all."

"It's too dangerous. What if it goes wrong?"

"It *won't*. We'll be really careful. And it's not like we're beginners anymore. We've learned lots already."

"We can do Glamour," said Rachel.

"Yeah!" Una was grinning with excitement now. "We are doing spells now. And, like Ms. Gold said, practice makes perfect."

Grace shook her head.

"Grace." Jenny took her arm. "By the time we've learned all the boring plants and stuff that Quinlan's teaching us, we'll be old enough to leave school. Do you want to get all the way to eighteen without casting any spells? Just think, if we can get the old coven back together, we'll have the best of both worlds. Lemon and Cat Lady can teach us all the theory they want, and Ms. Gold can show us how to use it."

Grace chewed on her lip and didn't answer.

"It's just looking into the past," Jenny pushed. "We're just going to watch people, like on TV."

"Come on, Grace," said Una. "Please."

Grace glanced at Adie, expecting to see a very worried face. But even Adie appeared unwilling to wait years to try out some real magic. Grace sighed.

"All right. But we have to be *really* careful."

✳ ✳ ✳

At lunchtime, the five girls went to the quietest part of the P block. Jenny had lit incense, and Grace was trying not to gag on the hideously floral scent.

"Do we need to have *four* sticks burning?"

"It's for atmosphere," Jenny replied. "It'll help."

"Not if they can smell it out in the hall."

Grace knew that wasn't likely, but she said it anyway. This part of the P block was generally empty during lunchtime, and they were safely hidden in one of the labs at the very end of the hallway.

The girls sat on the floor in a circle. In the center was Mrs. Quinlan's yearbook, a small dish filled with crushed herbs collected from the woods, and a sprinkling of soil from the football field. They each held a piece of silverware borrowed from home. A bracelet, a ring, a couple of forks, and, in Una's case, a very large soup ladle.

"That's huge!" said Rachel.

"My parents' wedding stuff is buried in the attic. I wasn't going digging through all that junk. This is fine."

"Let's get started." Jenny leaned forward, pushed her fork into the dish of herbs, and held on to it. The others followed suit, pushing their silverware into the herbs. Then they chanted:

"Beloved Chronos, lord of time,
Thy bounty and thy strength divine,
With meek and humble force we cast
This charm to view what now is past."

It wasn't long before something started happening.

The silverware started to jerk in their hands, making soft screeches against the porcelain dish. They each stared intently at the yearbook, careful not to let their minds wander. Grace felt that she could see right through the pages, down to the photograph of the old coven leaning against the wrought-iron gates.

And as she blinked, the picture came to life.

Vera slouched, glancing contemptuously at the camera. Beth leaned forward, looking up from beneath her heavy bangs. Meredith swept one hand beneath her golden locks and gripped the gate as the wind picked up, causing the metal hinges to rattle noisily. Grace could feel the wind in her face and hear the metallic sound continuing, but from much farther away. It picked up speed like an approaching train.

Clickety-click-click.

Clickety-click-click.

Grace held her breath as the image before her was swamped in light that spread while the metallic crunching got louder and louder. She fought to keep her concentration, her heart racing as she could almost feel the railroad ties beneath her, panting as the unseen train bore down on her, threatening to crush her. A foghorn blared and sent her flying across the floor. She blinked in the sudden silence.

There was soft grass against her cheek. She heard groaning as the others sat up and stretched their aching limbs. Looking up she could see a worn, gravel track through the grass, and beyond that, woods.

"What happened?" said Adie. "Where are we?"

"At school," Jenny replied.

"No, we were in the lab in the P block, doing the spell. Now, we're somehow outside."

"We're at school," Jenny said again, and pointed past Adie. Grace looked behind her to see what looked like the school building.

"That's not... It's different."

"There's no P block yet," said Jenny. "We are standing where the P block *will* be."

"Oh God. We've gone back in time!" said Grace.

She jumped to her feet and ran a few yards until she

could see the football field. Two teams were playing. One in blue, the other wearing a uniform that looked something like Saint John's. But subtly different.

"Oh God!" she said again. "It's actually happened!"

"Let's not panic," said Jenny.

"Let's not panic?" cried Grace. "Like TV, you said. We were supposed to be *watching*, that's all, not *in it*. You've taken us *back in time*."

"It's an old spell. I guess it's gotten really potent, like Mr. Pamuk said. Look, it's not permanent. We're bound to get bounced back to our own time."

"But when? We could be here for days. We could be here forever!"

"Stop panicking, Grace. You're not helping."

Grace blushed in spite of her anger. She didn't like being the one to lose her cool—even Adie wasn't screaming hysterically like Grace was. But she hated that Jenny didn't seem at all fazed that they'd just been zapped back to the 1970s. She tried to say this in calmer tones, but was interrupted by a loud ringing from inside the building. A door banged.

"You girls!" a woman's voice shrieked. "What do you think you're doing standing around outside? Get to your classes, immediately!"

A skinny figure marched toward them, swinging a heavy textbook.

"Didn't you hear me?" the woman said, the book quivering menacingly in her hand. "Get to your classes!"

Not knowing what else to do, the five girls obeyed and moved through the heavy doors into throngs of students. They circled the hallways, avoiding being pushed into classrooms by the crowds, until the halls were almost empty.

"What do we do?" asked Rachel.

"I don't know," said Grace. "But we better hide somewhere, or that woman might find us again."

"Vera!" called a voice nearby. "Wait for me!"

The girls all turned and, to their astonishment, saw a young Mrs. Quinlan, complete with red spiky hair and piercings, being chased by a young Ms. Lemon.

"Follow them," Una hissed, as the others were getting over the shock.

"They're going into a classroom," said Adie.

"So?"

"No," said Grace. "We can hide in the bathroom and wait 'til the bell rings. We'll follow them when they leave."

She grabbed Una's elbow and steered her toward the girls' bathroom.

"Do you hear that?" she heard Adie say behind her. Grace turned to answer, but Adie wasn't there. And Rachel wasn't there. And neither was Jenny.

"Una! Where'd they go?"

Before Una could answer, they were almost run over by a group of students and bundled through an open door.

"All right, everyone sit down and be quiet!" shouted the same skinny teacher, now wearing old-fashioned, thin-rimmed glasses. "Who are you two?"

Grace gulped.

"We're new," said Una, dragging Grace to a free desk.

The teacher stared at them for a long moment.

"Then sit down and pay attention."

Grace sat sweating in the front row. She could feel Una's foot jiggling nervously beside her.

"They can't have just disappeared," Una whispered.

"Well, they did. They were there one minute and gone the next."

"Detention for talking! See me after school!" The teacher glared at them above her spectacles. When she turned back to the board, Una whispered again.

"We have to get out of here. We have to find them."

"It's going to look a bit suspicious if we just get up and run out of the class."

"Then we'll do it stealthy like."

"We can't," said Grace.

"We've no choice. Ready?"

"What? Wait, what are—"

"Now!"

Grace watched in horror as Una slid beneath the desk and commando-crawled across the floor. Leaping to her feet, she swung the door open.

"Code red, Grace! Move, move, *move*!" she

yelled as she threw herself into the hallway and started running.

Grace went puce as the entire class turned to look at her. She glanced up at the openmouthed teacher apologetically.

"Um…"

Not knowing what else to do, she launched herself over the desk, landing painfully on her right ankle, and scrambled through the open door.

"What took you so long?" Una was panting at the end of the hallway.

Grace fought to catch her breath, then gasped and pointed as the teacher came thundering toward them.

"Fudge!" said Una, pushing through the exit. "Run!"

They tripped over each other as they raced back to the grassy area that would one day become the P block. There was still no sign of their friends, and the teacher wasn't giving up the chase.

"What do we do, Grace?"

"I don't know. Just let me think. Maybe they got pushed into one of the classrooms, like we did. Maybe—"

"What's that noise?" Una interrupted. "Do you hear that?"

Grace didn't hear the question. The dark clouds above them were threatening a storm, and the first of the rain had begun to fall. Blinking through the downpour, she could see a dark figure standing at the edge of the woods, watching them. She felt Una tug at her arm, and somewhere in the distance there was the metallic sound of a train coming.

Clickety-click-click.

Clickety-click-click.

The figure stood, cloaked in a black coat with the hood low. Grace squinted in the rain, trying to see the face.

Clickety-click-click.

Clickety-click-click.

She could make out the screech of the teacher behind her and Una's panicked voice begging her to run, but she couldn't take her eyes from the hooded figure.

Clickety-click-click.

Clickety-click-click.

Grace felt a rush through her body as the sound of the train filled her ears and a light began to grow in the air around her. The figure lifted its head and the hood pulled back just enough to reveal what was underneath.

Grace sucked in a breath, too terrified to scream. She felt Una grab hold of her as the light flashed bright, illuminating the man beneath the hood for a split second. Enough time for Grace to take in the pallid, withered face, with one blue eye and one white.

BAAAAAAARM!

Grace's skull pulsed with pain as the foghorn sound blared and faded. She felt warm arms wrap around her.

"Thank God!" said Adie. "We didn't know where you guys were!"

Blinking against her headache, Grace opened her eyes to see Adie's brow furrowed with worry. Una was fending off the coddling embraces of Rachel and Jenny.

"Where've you been?" said Jenny. "We bounced back here and you were just gone."

They were back in the safety of the P block lab with the dusty remains of the incense sticks scattered across the floor.

"It was totally crazy," said Una. "We saw a young Ms. Lemon and a young Cat Lady Quinlan with spiky red hair!"

"We were there for that part, Una," said Jenny.

"Oh yeah, sorry. Well, Grace and I got pushed into this classroom and then we had to make a break for it. Then we got chased by that teacher. She nearly had us. She was, like…and then we were…and then I could hear this train sound and then we totally disappeared! Bet she's freaking out right about now. Is it raining in here?"

"It *was* raining," Grace said, staring into space, "*there*."

"Grace?" Adie rubbed her arm. "Are you okay?"

"He was there. How was he there?"

"Who?"

Grace felt her hands tremble.

"The Mirrorman."

6

a blond bombshell

"Is it Cat Lady or Lemon tonight? I can't remember."
Jenny sighed as the girls headed to class.

"Mrs. Quinlan, I think," said Adie. "I'll check with
Ms. Lemon on the way to English."

"Ugh. Let's just skip it and go see Ms. Gold instead."

Grace didn't have the energy to explain why they
couldn't skip their theory lessons. The withered face
of the Mirrorman was burned on her memory, and she
just couldn't stop picturing the black cloak at the edge
of the woods.

"Whoops, sorry."

She barely noticed when James O'Connor bumped

into her, but blushed a bright pink when he smiled in apology before moving on.

"Hee, hee, hee," said Una. "Still hung up on him then?"

"Shut up, Una." Grace elbowed her arm, and Una's carton of orange juice squirted all over her sweater, making her squeal.

"Sorry," said Grace.

"No problem. Gives me a good reason to be late for class."

"Why don't you do a Glamour spell?" said Rachel.

"Me?" said Grace. "What for?"

"To get his attention. James's. You could make yourself look like Marilyn Monroe. He'd definitely ask you out then. Men go crazy for the Marilyn Monroe look. All blond hair and red lips."

"Why would I want to look like Marilyn Monroe? Then he wouldn't know it was me."

"Wonder if we can do that," Rachel mused. "Look *exactly* like someone else, I mean."

"See you, guys," said Adie, veering off to the A block.

"Tell Mr. Kilroy I'll be late," said Una. "Had an

incident with my orange juice. Make it sound like a disaster."

"Will do!"

Adie ducked past Mr. Kilroy as she headed to Ms. Lemon's classroom first. The door was slightly ajar and there were no students waiting outside. She tipped open the door and was about to call out when she caught sight of a small figure in a school uniform standing at the desk. The figure was rifling through an open drawer. Even stooped over, with her hair covering her face, Adie easily recognized Delilah's tiny frame. She watched as the small girl rummaged through papers, pulled out a wooden object on a leather cord, stared intently at it, then threw it back in.

"Waiting for me, Adie?"

Adie jumped at the sound of Ms. Lemon's voice behind her. Out of the corner of her eye, she saw Delilah do the same and quickly close the drawer.

"Um, yes, Miss. I was just checking if…if we've got a lesson later with you or—"

"You're with Vera this evening," the teacher replied, turning as Delilah walked out of her room with a timid smile. "Were you looking for me too?"

"Mr. Owens will be late for your department meeting today," Delilah almost whispered in her soft accent. "He said for me to tell you."

"Oh, well, thank you. You can head off to class now. You too, Adie."

Adie nodded in reply, catching the small girl's brown eyes for a moment as Delilah hurried down the hallway.

✳✳✳

Grace watched the seconds ticking by on the clock on the wall. Three minutes left. She hated English. Well, she didn't *hate* it. But she didn't *like* it. It was one subject she wasn't particularly good at, and that bothered her. She was mostly an A student, but in English she was a B. Stupid English.

"Erp!" Jenny slapped her hand over her own mouth.

Some heads turned their way.

"What is it?" Grace whispered.

"Don't look back."

Grace instinctively turned her head.

"I said *don't* look back!" Jenny hissed. "Okay, look back, but don't let anyone see you."

Confused, Grace pretended to scratch her neck, glancing toward the back of the classroom just long enough to catch a glimpse of platinum blond curls and ruby lips.

"Oh my *God*."

Sitting in the back row, with a pen held between her teeth and one hand absentmindedly twisting a strand of hair, was Marilyn Monroe.

"Why did she do that?" Grace gasped.

"Don't know," said Jenny. "But she's getting awesome at Glamour."

"Yeah, but why *now*? People are going to notice."

"She mustn't realize."

"We'll have to signal her somehow."

"How?" Jenny asked. "Without making anyone else look back?"

Grace pulled a hair tie from her pocket and twisted the eraser off the end of her pencil.

"You'll have to create a distraction," she said, "while I get her attention."

"What kind of distraction?"

"Anything. Just make sure you get people looking forward, not back. *Hurry*."

Grace tucked the eraser into one end of the hair tie and readied it to fire. There was a sudden whoosh of air beside her and a loud bang as Jenny leaped up onto the desk, pointing at a spot in front or her and shrieking.

"Rat! There's a rat!"

She stared and pointed frantically, as if following the creature to the front of the class. Other students began to squeal and a few climbed on tables.

"Jenny!" Mrs. Hennelly shouted. "Get down from there immediately."

"There's a rat, Miss!" Jenny's voice was still a high-pitched screech. "Right there. It's right near you, Miss!"

Mrs. Hennelly opened her mouth to speak again

but glanced nervously at the floor, eventually kneeling on her own chair, lifting both feet off the ground.

Grace swiftly turned, pulled the hair tie taut, and let the eraser fly. It smacked into Rachel's cheek and, luckily, the hysterical noise in the classroom covered her loud "Ow!"

She glared at Grace in confusion. Grace immediately pointed to her own face, pinched her cheeks, pouted her lips, and tugged at handfuls of her hair. Rachel stared at her for a moment before starting to touch her own face and hair. She jumped in realization and shook her head roughly to try and shake off the Glamour spell. Grace could see just a few strands of straight dark hair spilling out through the yellow curls and the ruby lips shrink a little, but that was it. The spell seemed stuck. Marilyn Monroe just wouldn't leave.

"More," Grace hissed at Jenny.

"What?"

"More," Grace repeated. "Give it a lot more. I've got to get Rach out of the classroom."

Jenny shrieked even louder at their teacher.

"Argh! Can't you *see* it, Miss?" she yelled.

By now, Mrs. Hennelly was on all fours on top of her desk.

"It's foaming at the mouth! I think it's got plague. Don't let it bite me, Miss!"

That was the last straw for the class. A few students bolted for the door, followed by everyone else. In the confusion, Grace grabbed hold of Rachel, pulled her sweater over her head, started running, and didn't stop until they reached the girls' bathroom.

"Shake it off, Rach!" she said.

"I'm trying!" said Rachel, her face red from the exertion.

Slowly, but surely, the Marilyn curls disappeared beneath sprouting strands of Rachel's dark hair, her lips lost their ruby tint, and the dark beauty spot beside her mouth faded into her porcelain skin.

"What was that?" said Grace. "What did you do that in class for? We could've been caught."

"I didn't know it had worked," Rachel replied,

still catching her breath. "I just did it quick. I wasn't even trying."

The door burst open, and Jenny marched in.

"That was *amazing*," she said, grinning.

Rachel smiled bashfully and shook her head.

"Sorry," she said, "I was just trying it out and—"

"Don't apologize," Jenny interrupted. "That was incredible. You're getting so good at it. You were totally Marilyn Monroe. Amazing!"

"Not *amazing*," said Grace sternly. "Dangerous. There's no way we could have explained that if anyone saw. Lucky you were stuck in the corner of class. I don't know how Mrs. Hennelly didn't spot you."

"I know, I'm sorry," Rachel replied.

"We have to be careful if we're going to go on trying out spells. I'm starting to think Mrs. Quinlan and Ms. Lemon were right."

"Oh, here we go," said Jenny, rolling her eyes. "What?"

"Siding with them again. They're not right, Grace.

They're just nervous about letting us have any control. They're afraid of what we can do."

"And they're right to be!" Grace's voice rose. "Have you forgotten how much trouble we caused last time, by summoning a demon?"

"No, I haven't forgotten." Jenny pursed her lips. "But it hasn't terrified me out of doing magic altogether. We got through that with flying colors. No one got hurt—"

"No one got *hurt*?"

"Not really, no."

"We nearly *killed* the Beast!"

"But we *didn't* kill her!" Jenny was shouting now. "We fixed it, the way we just fixed this. We'll make mistakes, Grace, but we have to make them so we can *learn*."

"This isn't learning. This is messing around, and it's really dangerous!"

"*Please* stop fighting," Rachel said suddenly.

She looked from Grace to Jenny, as they stared at each other.

"Look, you're both right," she said. "Yeah, it worked out as quite a cool spell, but there's no way I should even have attempted it in class. It was silly. I could've got us all in a lot of trouble."

Grace lowered her eyes and said softly, "I didn't mean to yell at you, Rach, it's just—"

"I know. You're looking out for us, and that's great. And Jenny just wants us to get better at magic, and that's great too. But I won't try any spells in class again, I promise."

"Well, just don't try them out at Mrs. Quinlan's tonight anyway," Grace said with a grin.

The other two smiled at the thought.

"No problem," said Rachel.

7

the mirrorman

The following afternoon, the girls were with Ms. Gold.

"Higher, girls, higher!" Ms. Gold cheered. "Don't stop now, you're doing so well!"

Grace couldn't watch. Every time she opened her eyes and saw the ground falling away beneath her, she had a flashback to that awful moment on the gabled roof of the shop that she and Adie had almost fallen from last year, the first time they'd tried to fly. Now she was flying again, as high as she dared—almost to the top branches of a sycamore—but she kept one arm outstretched, waiting to grab the branches if she should suddenly drop. Adie was just a few feet from her, also keeping her fingertips in among the leaves of a branch. Flying had been the most wonderful thing they had ever experienced, but it had already very nearly killed them both.

"Don't be so afraid, Grace and Adie," Ms. Gold called from the floor of the woods. "Let yourselves go. Be free!"

Grace pushed herself a little farther from the tree, but refused to go any farther. Una, despite her best efforts, hadn't gotten any higher than Grace and Adie. She flipped and swung awkwardly, grabbing at Grace's ankles as she tried to right herself.

"How do you get up straight?" she squealed. "I keep falling over."

"Tighten those core muscles," Ms. Gold called, "and keep your feet hip-width apart until you can hold your position."

As Una flailed below her, Grace could hear the happy shouts of Jenny and Rachel above. They'd flown very high into the sky, and Grace was nervous for them. They swooped and somersaulted, swinging each other around and letting go with shrieks of delight. She hoped the lesson would be over soon.

"All right, girls," their teacher shouted as Rachel and Jenny dropped down lower to listen. "I want to see how high you can go. Don't hold back, don't be afraid, just shoot as high as you dare."

Grace drifted a little above the sycamore tree before gliding down to the ground. She felt Adie land gently beside her, and Una landed in a heap at her feet. Above them, Rachel and Jenny were going higher and higher. They were so far away she could barely make them out; they were just specks in the sky. Silently, she begged them to come back down. After a few minutes, she could see Rachel moving smoothly down toward them, her dark hair fluttering in the wind.

"Couldn't beat her," she said as she landed with a grin. "She just kept on going."

Grace's stomach tightened in a knot. She looked at Ms. Gold, but the woman was staring up at the sky, a smile spreading across her luminous face.

Eventually, the tiny black dot in the sky grew and

grew until Grace could make out Jenny's shape. But something was wrong. She was going far too fast. She was no longer flying. She was falling.

Grace's heart leaped into her throat, and she grabbed hold of Ms. Gold's wrist. Above her, Jenny was plummeting, her hair whipping above her as she fell. Grace could hear screaming.

"No, Jenny, no!" Grace shook Ms. Gold's arm. "Do something! Save her!"

"Wait," the woman said, a smile still playing on her lips. "Just wait."

Grace looked up again in horror, Jenny's screams getting louder and louder. Until she realized they weren't screams. Jenny was whooping and shouting as she fell. She was dropping on purpose.

"Stop, Jenny! Slow down!"

The falling girl laughed and waited until the very last second before pulling up, only a few feet from the ground. She whooshed past her friends, sending torn plants and weeds flying in her wake. Then, soaring up into a wide backflip, she lowered herself gently to the ground.

"Impressive!" Ms. Gold was clapping feverishly. "Very impressive! You're fearless, Jenny, just fearless." She cupped Jenny's face in her hands. "A true witch."

Jenny blushed and grinned up at the golden teacher's smile.

Grace was silent as they trudged home through the woods. She felt physically sick after the shock of watching Jenny fall, and every time her friend laughed and joked about it, she fought the urge to reach out and slap her. She hurried past Ms. Gold and the others, afraid she might actually throw up.

"You okay?" Una said, catching up to her.

"Fine."

"You don't look fine. You're really white."

Grace bit back tears and kept walking.

"Is it because Jenny's doing really well at the magic stuff?" said Una. "You don't have to worry about that. *You're* good at lots of stuff. And you'll get better. We all will. Sure, look at me. I spent the whole lesson with my feet in the air!"

"Una, it's not that—"

Grace stopped suddenly. She could hear something in the distance. It was getting closer. A metallic sound.

Clickety-click-click.

Clickety-click-click.

"Do you hear that?" said Grace. "Sounds like a train."

Una shook her head.

"It's getting closer."

Clickety-click-click.

Clickety-click-click.

"Oh no!"

"Grace? No, it can't be." Una put her hands to her face and kept shaking her head.

"Una, I'm scared." She reached out to grab her friend, but suddenly the sound was upon her.

Clickety-click-click.

Clickety-click-click.

Grace squinted against the bright flash of light and the thunderous foghorn blast, covering her ears as she fell to her knees. When she opened her eyes, she was alone in the dark.

The air was cold, and she was breathing mist. She could feel the crackling of twigs and leaves beneath her as she slowly got to her feet. The woods were so quiet even her breath seemed too loud. She fought to slow her breathing and mute the sound, but that made the silence even worse. Stepping in the direction of the school, she winced at the noise she made. It seemed like every creature in the woods was listening to her, watching her. In the dim light of the stars even the trees looked sinister, stretching their black branches out to catch her hair and scratch her skin. She remembered her frightening experience in the stone house, when she had waited in the dark for the trapped souls that had whispered and screamed. Alone in the derelict bungalow, she remembered the punches coming out of nowhere, invisible hands and fists that beat her and drew blood.

Grace moved as quickly as she dared. But as she neared the edge of the woods, there was a flicker of movement to her right. She froze. There, not too far from her, was something blacker than the dark.

She stared and stared until…there, it moved again. It wasn't an animal. Its surface was black and glossy. A black raincoat. With a hood.

Grace ran. She ran as if her life depended on it. The entrance to the woods was just ahead of her. Beyond that she could see the outline of the school building. She could hear the Mirrorman behind her. His feet pounded in time with hers; his breathing was loud and coarse. His coat made a *shish shish* sound as he chased her.

Her legs were burning as she rounded the school gates. Through the glass hallway, there was a hint of light. There was someone still in the school. If she could get there, she'd be safe.

There was a grunt in his breathing now as they sprinted toward the door. Grace ignored the increasing pain in her legs and smacked through the doorway, turning just in time to avoid his grasping hand and bolting toward the light.

The light was coming from the library. As she burst through the door, she threw a glance over her shoulder.

Nothing. He was gone.

"This isn't a game," a voice was saying from deep inside the library. "This *anomaly* of yours—we don't know what force we could pull out of there. It could kill us all!"

Grace ducked down to her haunches and peeked around a bookcase. The young Mrs. Quinlan—Vera—sat on a desk with one foot on a chair and one elbow leaning on her knee. Grace was back in 1977.

"So what, we just ignore it?" Meredith Gold was opposite her, pacing impatiently. "It's an area of *intense* magic, right here in the school! We were *meant* to find it, Vera, don't you get it? This is what we're here for."

"*Meant* to find it? Would you listen to yourself? God, Meredith, you're such a child."

"We don't even know what's down there." Grace had almost missed Beth Lemon, who sat half-hidden behind Vera, with her long bangs covering one eye. "The edge is burning with energy."

"Then let's find out!" Meredith threw her hands in the air in exasperation.

"We *are* finding out," said Vera.

"With stupid Parsing spells and energy enchantments? Why not just sit there with a clipboard and a pen for all *that's* worth?"

"You're talking about opening up this world to another *realm*."

"I'm talking about picking up the box and giving it a shake!" said Meredith. "Let's see what comes out."

Vera kicked her boot off the chair and stood, turning her back to Meredith as she adjusted her piercings and pulled her denim jacket closed.

"We'll keep going with Beth's invocations and get as much information as we can. End of story."

Meredith stared coldly at the back of Vera's head and didn't reply. Grace was so intent on the scene in front of her, she almost didn't hear it. A gentle *shish shish* sound behind her.

Slowly Grace looked back over her shoulder. There he was, just a few yards away behind a bookcase, his hooded coat blacker than the dark.

Grace jumped to her feet and ran out of the door

toward the main hall. She could hear her own heart thudding and the sound of the Mirrorman right behind her. But there was that other noise again— that familiar metallic sound.

Clickety-click-click.

Clickety-click-click.

Grace rounded the corner into the hall, skidding on the linoleum and sliding onto all fours. She yelped as she felt a rush of air at the back of her neck and his hand just missing her as she lunged forward in the dimness.

Clickety-click-click.

Clickety-click-click.

Where was the foghorn? She wasn't safe until it sounded. Ahead of her, Grace could see the turnoff to the staff room. She swerved to make the corner and felt hands grabbing her and tightening around her waist. She was wrenched backward and spun around. The Mirrorman grabbed a handful of her collar, and she was forced to look up into the pasty, withered face. In the gloom his white eye glowed. His thin lips parted to reveal blackened teeth and gums.

"You don't belong here," said a dead, flat voice.

Grace's scream mingled with the blasting foghorn sound, and she was blinded by piercing white light. Then she was falling.

Grace smacked onto the floor, face-first, and pain gushed through her. She groaned, cupping her sore cheek, then looked up. On the wall there were framed pictures of the school that she recognized. They were of kids she recognized, in uniforms she recognized. She was back in her own time. And she was alone.

Except that she wasn't. As Grace climbed to her feet, using a bench to steady her weak knees, a withered hand gripped the corner of the wall. As she pushed off the bench and headed, limping, for the exit, a pair of eyes watched her leave, one blue, one white.

8
out in the cold

"*La circulation.*"

"*La circulation*, traffic. Very good, Grace."

Ms. Lemon turned to scrawl the words across the board.

"Hey," Jenny hissed, giving Grace a nudge. "Are you not talking to me?"

Grace feigned a casual indifference and shook her head.

"'Course not. I mean, of course I'm talking to you."

She didn't look at Jenny, just pretended to concentrate on the whiteboard. She hadn't told the others about the Mirrorman, and she was jumpy. Why *her*? Why was *she* the one hurtling back in time? And when was it going to happen again? When Adie had clicked her pencil case shut, Grace practically leaped out of her skin.

"You haven't talked to me at all since yesterday," Jenny went on. "Are you mad at me or something?"

"I'm not mad"—Grace finally turned to look at her—"I'm just... Wait, where'd you get that necklace?"

Jenny grinned and fingered the bronze charm at her neck.

"Ms. Gold gave it to me. Cool, isn't it?"

Grace bit back a pang of jealousy. After all, it had been Jenny who'd insisted on doing the stupid time-travel spell in the first place. And now she was getting rewards for flying dangerously.

"Did you get that because you won the flying game?"

"No, just 'cause. She says I've got great potential. That I'm fearless—the most important trait a witch can have." Jenny fingered the pendant again. "She says I'm meant for great things."

Grace didn't answer. Jenny dropped the charm and frowned.

"I *knew* it. You *are* mad at me."

"I'm not!"

"Because of the flying, is that it? Because I'm better at it than you?"

"No, because you scared me."

"It's because I was better than you," said Jenny. "You're just jealous because I'm the best at witchcraft!"

Grace's face felt hot.

"I'm *not* jealous! And it was only the flying you were good at. Rachel's a much stronger Glamourer than you. We'll all be good at different things. We just haven't tried them all yet."

"And what if there isn't even one thing you're good at?" Jenny whispered. "What if you're *never* a great witch? Will you stop talking to all of us? You'll be a little Mrs. Quinlan then, won't you?"

Grace sucked in breath and opened her mouth to retort, but the words stuck in her throat.

"Jenny," Ms. Lemon said suddenly. "Repeat what I just said."

Jenny didn't answer but continued to stare at Grace.

"Jenny!" the teacher said, louder this time. "I asked you to repeat what I just said to the class."

"I wasn't listening," Jenny replied, slowly looking forward and folding her arms.

"Excuse me?"

"I said I wasn't listening."

There was silence as Ms. Lemon waited for more. Finally, her cheeks flushed a little and she frowned.

"All right, then get to Mr. Collins's office," she said. "I don't want to see you for the rest of the class."

Jenny gave her a pointed look, then pushed her chair back, stood up, and left the room. Grace's eyes were too full of tears to see properly, but she could feel the teacher's gaze on her.

✳✳✳

Delilah sat on the stones steps at one side of the school building and chewed quietly on half of Grace's sandwich.

"She thinks I'm mad at her over...something," said

Grace from the step above. "But I'm not. And I'm not jealous either."

The small girl looked up at her with her puppy-dog eyes and said nothing.

"Well, maybe just a *little* bit jealous. A *tiny* bit. She always jumps in feetfirst, and I'm always a little more scared and really careful. But you have to be careful, otherwise…"

Grace sighed and looked down at the girl perched below. It was easy to talk to someone who hardly said anything at all. She smiled and handed Delilah the other half of her sandwich.

"Do you want it? I don't feel like eating it right now."

The girl took it and smiled. Watching her eat hungrily with her head down and her hair covering her face, Grace wondered.

"Delilah," she said, "you were there when Jenny broke the window, weren't you?"

The small girl's jaw stopped moving, and she stared into her sandwich.

"Did you…?" Grace wasn't sure how to ask. "Did you see what happened?"

Delilah began chewing again, picking off tiny pieces of crust and dropping them on the ground.

"You saw, didn't you?" said Grace.

The small girl nodded.

"You didn't say anything to us."

The girl shook her head.

"Did you tell anyone else?"

Another shake of the head.

"Weren't you curious? Don't you want to know about Ms. Gold? And us?"

Delilah shrugged shyly and continued picking at the sandwich. Grace thought that felt like a *yes*, but didn't know how to reply. Finally, Delilah lifted her chin and said, "It's like magic."

Grace smiled and nodded, but the girl suddenly shouldered her bag and stood up.

"I have to go," she said.

"What? But lunch isn't over yet. We've still got another ten minutes."

"I have to go," Delilah said again, turning and hurrying away, leaving Grace staring after her.

"Hey, you okay?"

Grace looked behind her to see Adie's friendly smile.

"Yeah, I'm fine. Just wanted some fresh air, that's all."

"How come she took off so fast?" Adie said, nodding in Delilah's direction.

"Don't know," Grace replied. "Did Jenny ask you to find me?"

"No. But we all missed you at lunch. We haven't really talked since you got bounced back in time again. Are you sure you're okay?"

Grace nodded quickly.

"Poor Una really freaked out." Adie smiled. "Must be the remnants of the spell wearing off or something. I don't know why it's just you, but I'm sure it won't happen again. Jenny and the others really want to hear about it. Why don't you come back in before the bell rings?"

"No. Thank you."

Adie sighed.

"You both said things you didn't mean."

"*I* didn't," Grace exclaimed. "She was the one acting all full of herself."

"She's just excited, that's all. We all are. We're doing *real* spells, and they're actually working."

Grace didn't reply.

"Please come in. You're not going to sit out here every lunchtime on your own, are you?"

"I wasn't on my own."

"You should be with your friends."

"Delilah is our friend."

Adie bit her lip and didn't answer.

"Why don't you like her?" said Grace. "She's really nice, and she's having a hard time at school."

"I know, it's just, she's a bit…"

"A bit what?"

"A bit strange, that's all. I'm just not sure about her." Adie held Grace's eyes with a pleading look.

"Well, I am," Grace said, getting to her feet. "You should go back to Jenny and the others. I'll see you later."

Grace pretended she didn't see Adie's hand reach for her as she walked away.

***

Shish shish, shish shish.

Grace could see the exit from the woods ahead. She was nearly there, just a few more yards.

Shish shish, shish shish.

There was light outside the woods, like daylight. But in among the trees she was still in the dark. Just a few steps more and she'd be safe. But her feet were sticky. She was slowing down. The ground was turning to molasses underneath her, sucking at her shoes and swallowing her ankles. She dropped to all fours, grabbing at the brown mulch and dragging her body forward. But it wasn't enough. She sank deeper still, unable to pull her knees free. The daylight in front seemed miles away, the darkness stretching out farther and farther until the light was just a pinpoint in the distance. There was a rush of air, then a clawing at her neck. She looked back at the gilded frame, twisted around broken shards of glass. The Mirrorman leaned out of it, his mouth gaping horribly wide. His hands reached for her face.

"No!"

Grace wrestled with the bedspread until her arms were gently held down and she heard her mother's voice.

"It's all right, sweetheart. It's just a dream."

Grace stopped struggling as her eyes focused in the dim light of her bedroom. Her hair was plastered to her forehead and her heart was racing.

"It's all right, sweetheart," her mom said again.

Sitting up, Grace stretched out her fingers, which looked clean and white. But she could almost feel remnants of the sticky ground between them.

"That must have been some nightmare," her mother said, tucking strands of damp hair behind her ears. "What was it about?"

The image of the Mirrorman stretching out of the broken mirror was still clear in Grace's mind, his mouth distended and hideous, his clawed hands grasping for her. She shuddered and shook her head.

"I don't remember."

When her mother had left the room, leaving a cup

of warm milk by her bedside, Grace lay wide-awake. She wriggled her fingers, trying to dispel the grainy feeling of earth between them.

Shish.

She stopped.

Shish shish.

Fear prickled her skin. The sound was coming from somewhere in front of her, but all she could see was the dim outline of her desk.

Shish shish.

A book slid from the desk, all by itself, and hit the carpet with a soft thump. Minutes passed before Grace could move. Finally, she steeled her nerves. Slipping her feet onto the floor, she shuffled forward, placed trembling fingers on one corner of the book, and pulled it toward herself. It was Mrs. Quinlan's yearbook, open on a large photograph of the school football field.

Grace scrutinized the old photo. Boys in team jerseys hugged each other and punched their fists in the air in victory; one of them had been hoisted onto the others' shoulders. The ground beneath them was mucky, and their shoes and socks and the ball at their feet were all covered in mud. The sky was overcast, but it didn't look like it was raining. In the background she could see the hedge that led to Mrs. Quinlan's street. And something else. Some*one* else. Right at the end of the field. He held a rake in one hand and a black bag in the other. A pile of leaves reached to his knees just below his black, hooded coat. He was looking right into the camera, right at *her*.

Grace slammed the book shut and threw herself under the duvet, pulling it all the way over her head.

✳✳✳

Standing between Adie, Rachel, and Una in the middle of the A block, Grace couldn't miss the doubtful glances they gave each other.

"Why didn't you tell us about it before?" asked Rachel.

"I—I don't know," Grace stammered. "I was mad at Jenny after the flying thing and…I just didn't."

She looked at each of them, and they weren't even trying to hide the doubt anymore.

"What?"

"You know that you don't need some big emergency to keep us around," Adie said gently. "We're always here."

"What do you mean?" said Grace. "You think I'm lying?"

Adie cleared her throat nervously and shook her head.

"No, no," she said, "I'm only saying that Mirrorman or no Mirrorman, we're always your friends."

"Why don't you believe me? I'm not making this up."

"It's all right," Una said, putting one hand on her arm. "We do believe you."

The pitying look on her face told Grace the truth. She couldn't understand why they thought she would make up such a horrible story. She regretted keeping it to herself for so long. Just then, as if she wasn't miserable enough, Grace saw Jenny come strolling down the hallway with James O'Connor.

"Hey, Grace," said Jenny, beaming.

"Hi, Jenny," Grace replied quietly.

"I was just telling James about Ms. Gold." Jenny grinned up at James confidently. "She's the best teacher ever."

"You're not even in her class," said Grace.

Jenny turned her eyes to Grace but spoke to James.

"A few of us are taking some extra after-school classes with her."

"Extra geography classes?" James said with surprise. "Who'd want to do that?"

"Oh, not geography. Nonschool subjects only." Jenny put her finger to her lips and leaned toward him, whispering. "But, shush. It's a secret."

James gave a little laugh as his cheeks reddened. Just then, the school bell rang.

"We better get to class," said Adie, as they all turned to make their way up the hallway.

"Sure thing," said Jenny. "Oh, James?"

"Yeah?" he said, turning back to her.

"Do you want to catch a movie on Saturday? That new horror one's supposed to be great."

Grace felt her heart drop into her shoes.

"Um…" James stammered, his rosy cheeks going redder.

"Eight o'clock at the Omniplex," Jenny said firmly. "I'll see you just outside, okay?"

"Er…okay, sure," he said with a shy smile. "See you there."

Grace watched him shrug his bag onto his shoulder and make his way up the hallway. There was an uncomfortable silence as Rachel, Una, and Adie looked first at Jenny, then at Grace, not sure what they were supposed to say.

"All righty," Jenny said, as if nothing had happened. "Let's go."

She marched down the hall without looking back. Grace half expected the others to let her go on alone, but after a few sympathetic glances in her direction, they followed Jenny to class. Only Adie spoke to her.

"You okay?"

Grace nodded, but she wasn't okay. And she didn't know what hurt most—that one of her best friends was going out with the boy she liked, or that none of her other best friends had said anything about it. She'd never felt so alone.

By the time they reached the C block, anger had overtaken hurt. In the doorway Grace grabbed Jenny by the elbow and pulled her aside.

"What's gotten into you?" she demanded. "Why are you being so mean?"

"What the hell are you talking about?"

"You know exactly what I'm talking about. You… you asked out James O'Connor, just to get at me!"

Jenny looked at her with fake confusion.

"How was *I* supposed to know you liked him?" she said.

"You've known for ages that I like him. You've teased me about it lots of times," said Grace.

"Well, I presumed you were over that. I mean, if you liked him so much, why didn't you ever ask him out?"

Grace stared at her, watching the smugness spread across Jenny's brow.

"That would be a bit unfair, don't you think?" Jenny said, softly pushing Grace backward and heading back to the classroom door. "You never going out with a boy, but never letting anyone else go out with him either." She turned into the room and paused to speak over her shoulder. "If you want something, maybe next time you shouldn't wait so long to do something about it."

9

a history

Past the woods and across the rickety old bridge, Grace hurried to keep pace with Delilah. There were no street-lights this far out of town and it was dark and quiet. There were no paths either, once they crossed the river, so they had to walk along the side of the road with the rushing water loud to their left and the mucky ground to their right swelling up onto a hill with more woods. There were a few isolated birdcalls still sounding out, even though the sun had gone down. Grace had to concentrate to keep her footing at the edge of the pavement, but the small girl in front of her walked fast, with her head up, as if in broad daylight.

About fifteen minutes later they reached a turnoff that ran around the base of the hill. The road narrowed, and the pavement turned into a mess of gravel and mud. There was a wall of trees on either side, blocking out what little light the moon provided. Grace grabbed the tip of one strap on Delilah's bag and trusted the girl to lead her safely down the track.

When they reached the end of the road, Grace was sure they had made a mistake. They stood in front of a dilapidated structure that could only be referred to as a barn, not a house. There was no light inside or outside the building, the windows were cracked, the wooden slats that covered it were split and rotting, and it was surrounded by woodland that had to be impassable in bad weather.

"Are you sure your mother won't mind me coming over?" Grace whispered.

"She won't mind," Delilah replied. "She's never here anyway."

Grace wasn't surprised. If she lived here, she wouldn't want to come home either.

She followed Delilah up the two steps that led to the porch; the wooden planks felt spongy beneath her feet. The small girl bent down to pick up an old-fashioned oil lamp, which she lit with some matches pulled from her pocket. Her face illuminated as she twisted the brass key until the flame was at its brightest. Holding the lamp by her cheek, she turned the black handle and the door opened with an echoing creak.

The inside of the house was as welcoming as the outside. There was the bare minimum of furniture, and no lighting or radiators that Grace could see. She pulled up the collar on her jacket and shivered against the freezing cold. As Delilah led her to the kitchen at the back of the house, there was a growing sickly sweet smell of rotting food mixed with the damp of the wood. Everything was grimy and growing mold, and there was the constant sound of tiny scurrying feet in the walls and under the floorboards.

Delilah dropped her bag onto the table and pulled up two chairs. The table, made out of planks roughly nailed together, looked as rotten as the rest of the house. Grace didn't want to sit at it but, out of politeness, she took the offered chair and sat, holding her schoolbag in her lap.

"I don't know what we need," said Delilah.

"I have everything here," Grace said, opening her bag and placing several items on the table. "A couple of silver forks. There's one each. A porcelain dish, and the soil and herb blend. I just hope there's enough. I could only find a tiny bit of Green Figwort."

"What's that?" said Delilah, pointing.

"Incense." Grace had forgotten she'd brought it. She motioned for Delilah's matches, thankful for the vanilla scent that masked the stench of the decaying house.

"How does the spell work?" asked Delilah, picking up a silver fork.

"We hold the silver in the dish with the blend, and then I say the spell. I've written a new verse, so it won't be as potent as the last one. We *should* just be able to watch past events from here."

Grace had double-checked and knew she was right

about the potency, but there was still a swarm of butterflies growing in her stomach.

"Are you sure you want to do this?" she said, holding her fork above the dish. "You don't have to."

Delilah's brown eyes smiled, and she nodded her head.

"Thanks," said Grace, "for helping me."

She pulled a piece of paper from her jacket pocket and unfolded it, laying it flat on the table. It was the figure of the Mirrorman, cut out of Mrs. Quinlan's yearbook. She stuck the end of her fork into the blend, and Delilah did the same. Then Grace started to chant:

"God of time, we ask this blessing,
Save us all this woeful guessing,
Break this old man's mystery,
And show us his dark history."

Grace kept her focus on the picture until she heard a bubble-popping sound. Then another. At the center of the wooden table, a dark liquid was filling the narrow gaps between the planks. It bubbled and spat, then bubbled some more until it spilled over the boards, reaching out with fluid fingers that turned to meet each other and form a wide, wet circle. The surface smoothed out until the girls could see their own reflections. Then there was a "plop," like someone had dropped a pebble into the middle of the puddle and ripples spread from the center, revealing an image of a grand house surrounded by gardens.

A young boy plays with a slingshot, taking out wildflower heads as they sway in the breeze. The boy stops suddenly, staring ahead and, as the view pans out, there is an old woman approaching him from the adjoining woods. He turns and runs away, back toward the grand house where a middle-aged man is standing. Their clothes are old-fashioned, like Grace has seen in history books at school. The old woman reaches the house, where the man waits, the boy hiding behind his legs.

"There will be no more talk," the man says gruffly. "A notice of eviction has been served."

"I wish to give you one more chance," the woman says. "One last chance to save your souls. My home is my own, and I have lived there since I was a child. I ask only for my small plot and nothing more."

"Your plot," the man replies, "is in the center of what will be new farmland, to be sold. Be gone by tomorrow or I will have the bailiffs throw you out and burn every last one of your possessions."

The woman stands motionless. A small hump beneath her woolen shawl wriggles, and a young red squirrel peeps out. It scampers up the woman's arm to perch on her shoulder.

"By tomorrow," says the woman, "you will be sorry."

From the folds of her clothes she pulls a parcel made of sackcloth. Dropping it at the man's feet, she stamps on it with one foot and twists her heel into it until a foul-smelling slime oozes out between the threads and seeps into the ground.

"As you sow," she shrieks, raising her hands in the air, "so shall you reap!"

"Get off my land!" the man shouts.

Emboldened by his father's anger, the boy pulls his slingshot taut and fires a stone at the squirrel on the woman's shoulder. It hits the animal in the eye, and the squirrel falls lifeless to the ground. The woman screams, grasping the creature in her clawed hands and holding it to her cheek. A few terrible sobs escape her mouth before she turns, and only then is her whole face visible. Her eyes burn with hate, her skin is blighted and raw, her teeth are scarce, and the few she has are black and loose. The boy ducks behind his father, gripping his coat, but the woman doesn't rush at him.

"As you sow," she whispers, "so shall you reap."

She lifts up the end of her shawl, wraps it around the squirrel, and cradles it in her arms. Then, turning her back on them, she leaves the grounds and disappears into the woods.

Ripples wash away the image. As they clear, the image shows the same boy, this time tossing and turning in bed. He wakes suddenly and screams and screams. He doesn't stop even when his mother and father come running to his room. His mother grabs his shoulders and soothes him, then screams herself. His left eye has gone from blue to pearly white. The father is distraught and immediately blames the old woman for taking half his son's sight. He sends the bailiffs to burn her out of her home, but they refuse, pleading fear and telling stories of monstrous beasts and angry spirits.

Enraged, the father summons his men from the fields and commands them to dam the river and cut off her water supply. Another wash of ripples reveals the father drinking cup after cup of water. His skin looks yellow and dry. He is weak but won't stop to eat. He drinks and drinks but can't seem to quench his thirst.

The image switches to the mother riding on

horseback into the woods and carrying her husband's gun. She finds the hut with two goats tethered outside, but the woman is not there. Incensed, she loosens the ropes that bind the animals and chases them off, bellowing into the twilight that the old woman must pay for her crimes.

More ripples in the puddle and the image now is of the family's herd of cows stampeding through gates that aren't strong enough to hold them. Farmhands are trampled as the cattle run. The animals disappear over the horizon, leaving a path of destruction behind them. The father and several crooked-looking men go into the woods with guns, knives, and flaming torches and set fire to old woman's roof. The woman escapes, but her hut is burned to cinders.

This image is blurred slightly by the smoking cinders, which then become the burning embers of another house—the grand house of the boy and his parents. The family stand in the blackened gardens as the father's men throw useless buckets of water on what is left of their home. The father takes the hands of his wife and son and leads them into the woods. He falls to his knees in front of the woman, who sits on a stool in the ashes of her home. He begs her forgiveness. He offers her ownership of her plot. He cries and tells her his family have suffered enough.

The old woman stands and says his family has not suffered as she has suffered, but that they soon will. A startled cry from the mother makes the father turn around. Their son has disappeared. When they turn back, the old woman is also gone.

One last ripple across the puddle of water, and the old woman sits on a stool by the fire. An Irish wolfhound lies by her feet sleeping. A bird calls outside the hut and the dog jerks awake. He listens intently before resting his head on his paws once again and closing his unusual eyes, one blue, one milky white.

*** ***

Grace and Delilah watched as the liquid drained through the boards and the last image faded to nothing.

"Is that *it*?" asked Grace. "What happened then? How did he become human again? Oh, I knew there wasn't enough Green Figwort!"

Delilah traced her finger through the damp remains on the table and didn't seem to hear.

"Delilah?" said Grace. "Are you freaked out?"

The girl dried her finger on her sweater and shook her head, smiling.

"No, it's cool. It's really magic!"

Grace sighed. She didn't know how serious it was for her to have told Delilah about her friends and their spells. Had she now brought Delilah into their coven without asking anyone? Would Ms. Lemon be angry? Would Mrs. Quinlan? She didn't know the answers, but at least the girl hadn't lost it when she saw the magic happening for real. Besides, if her friends thought she was making up stories about the Mirrorman, who else could she turn to for help?

10
the hound

Grace sat cross-legged at the edge of the football field with the evening dew soaking into her school uniform. She didn't sit apart from Jenny and the others, but was at an angle so she didn't have to look any of them in the eye.

"Witches," said Ms. Gold, with her eyes closed, "are fond of familiars. They consist of two types: either animal companions that are smarter than the average dog or cat, or Metamorphs—"

"People that have been turned into an animal form," said Grace.

Ms. Gold opened her eyes for a moment.

"Yes. Cursed humans. The smarter-than-average animal is bound to the witch by *devotion*. It protects her, warns her of danger, keeps her company, and is very much like a pet. But the Metamorph is bound to the witch by *magic*. She commands its obedience, and it has to comply."

"For how long?" asked Grace.

"For as long as the witch lives," the teacher replied. "It is possible for a witch to release a metamorphic familiar from its curse before her death, but I've never heard of it done. When a witch curses a human being, it is generally for good reason."

"Do you have a familiar?" said Jenny, glancing at Ms. Gold before closing her eyes and lifting her chin to mirror the woman's posture.

"I do not," the teacher replied. "I have never favored familiars. Animals require feeding, cleaning, and don't travel well."

"Plus, I bet you've never cursed anyone to be your Metamorph slave," Una said with a giggle.

"That too," said Ms. Gold, smiling.

"So you just never have an animal companion at all?" asked Rachel.

"I very often have an animal companion," said Ms. Gold. "And that leads us to our next spell—Origination. When I feel like company, protection, or just the desire to see something beautiful, I create a companion."

"Like the golden butterflies," said Una.

"Correct. They fill the air with beauty as I perform such routine and menial tasks as collecting flora and fauna. They make the time pass so much more pleasantly."

"Can we create them first? Oh, please, please, please!"

Ms. Gold smiled and swept a hand beneath her golden locks.

"They are a little complicated," she said. "Each creature requires Origination. We start with one and go from there. As you improve, you will be able to create two at a time, three, then four. Origination of thousands requires proficiency that only comes from hundreds of hours of practice."

Her hand glided over the grass by her knees, her fingers occasionally squeezing to pluck the tip off a single blade.

"For Origination you need a life template— something that is, or was, living. The presence of wood or paper can be enough, but something that is still alive makes the job much easier. That's why we're sitting directly on the ground here, surrounded by plant and tiny animal life. You can't possibly be without a life template here because life is all around you."

She rested her palms on her knees and continued.

"Your training up to this point has been about focusing your mind. Whether you know it or not, exercising your magical muscles has strengthened them and improved your concentration. Simple spells you once found difficult will become easier and easier as time goes on. This enchantment requires, above all, concentration. Choose one living thing, one blade of grass, one flower, one insect, which- ever you prefer. But only one. This will be your life template. The benefit of your surroundings is that if your mind or eye should slip even slightly, you may be able to grab the next template before the moment of Origination occurs."

The girls gazed at their teacher, enraptured.

"Now, relax and focus," she said. "Choose a template and direct all your attention to it; don't drift. Stare at the object until everything around it blurs, and repeat after me, *Ex vita vetera, vita nova.*"

The girls repeated the words together in a soft drone.

"You will feel a pumping behind your eyes," said Ms. Gold. "Don't be alarmed. In a few seconds, that will become slightly painful, which is also perfectly normal."

Slightly painful was an understatement. Grace found it difficult to keep her concentration on her blade of grass as little shards of pain darted through her eyeballs. As the stinging continued, the grass in her hand ballooned and warped.

"Your template is now yours to copy." Ms. Gold's voice was so smooth it made Grace feel drowsy. "I want you to envisage a sphere closing around your template. Pull the sphere away from that spot and place your copy on the ground. Picture your desired animal inside the sphere, and be as *detailed* as you can. When you feel it is solid, open the sphere and greet your new companion."

Grace pictured a small lizard with light green skin and a blue fringe along its spine. It was weird, not being able to see the animal behind the sphere's surface, but being able somehow to feel it take shape. When she was sure it was complete, she willed the sphere to split in two.

Sitting on the grass in front of her was her little lizard. His tiny toes were cushioned with circular pads, his eyes were bright and black, and the fringe down his back was a startling shade of blue. She gasped in delight and looked at the others. Each of them was staring at her own animal. Rachel's sleek black cat stretched forward, winding its tail around her finger-tips and eyeing Adie's bluebird, which flitted from her knee to her shoulder. Poor Una looked aghast at the hybrid creature squirming by her ankles. The head, shoulder, and one arm were that of a monkey, while the bottom half appeared to be that of a small deer. She started to cry.

"I couldn't decide," she sobbed, reaching out to soothe the flailing thing, but not knowing how.

"Don't worry, Una," said Jenny. "It's not like it's real."

"Jenny's right," said Ms. Gold. "It's just a figment of your imagination that can be dismissed as easily as it is created. It can't suffer."

"It *looks* like it's suffering," said Adie.

Ms. Gold smiled and waved her hand.

"Dismiss it, Una. That's all you have to do."

Una raised her hand and hesitated, gazing down at the monkey-deer with wet eyes.

"Sorry," she whispered, then waved her arm roughly. The creature opened its mouth as if to cry out and popped into nothingness. Una didn't take her eyes from the empty space.

The others stayed quiet, not wanting to make too much of their own cute companions when Una's had been so disastrous. But Grace couldn't help feeling a swell of pride at her little lizard, Adie's bluebird, and Rachel's cat. When she looked for Jenny's companion, though, she could only see a large, black mound.

"What's yours, Jenny?" said Rachel.

Jenny smiled as the mound rose to stand on its thick black legs. It was a massive dog with caked skin instead of fur. Its face was short and mean, and its red eyes glinted wickedly in the fading light of the sun.

"It's hideous." The words were out of Grace's mouth before she realized.

The smile vanished from Jenny's face.

"It's the Hound of the Baskervilles," she said, holding Grace's eye.

"It's extraordinary," breathed Ms. Gold. "Really, Jenny, you've outdone yourself. It's an exquisite example of natural skill."

"It won't go for the others, will it?" Rachel wrapped an arm around her cat.

Ms. Gold laughed and rubbed her palms together.

"That," she said, "is the second lesson of Origination.

To create an animal is one thing. To maintain control of it is another. A real witch is *fearless*. The animal is yours. It must obey your will. So command it. Don't be afraid."

As if to demonstrate her point, the black cat sprang out of Rachel's arms toward the bluebird, with claws outstretched. Adie squealed and spun around, shielding the bird as the cat bounced off her back and slunk to the ground, stealthily creeping around her body for another attempt.

"Rachel!" Adie shouted.

"Sorry, Adie," said Rachel, grabbing the cat's hindquarters and draping it over her shoulder. "Stop messing, you. Be good."

"Don't *tell* it what to do," said Ms. Gold. "It's a part of you. *Will* it to behave."

Rachel scrunched up her face as the cat squirmed and meowed. As she and Adie struggled to keep their companions apart, Grace placed her hand on the ground and willed the lizard to walk forward. The animal obediently padded onto her palm and settled himself in a little coil. She gently stroked his head and smiled as he nudged her fingertips for more petting at the end of each stroke.

A deep, guttural sound interrupted the moment. The hound had turned to face her and was breathing heavily, its red eyes latched on the lizard in her hand. Horrified, she cupped her companion to her chest.

"Jenny," she said. "Please make it stop."

Jenny was staring at the back of the dog and didn't reply. The animal exhaled with a snort, like a bull about to charge.

"Jenny!" Grace cried.

The hound lunged forward, its speed belying its huge size, and Grace rolled out of its path, barely managing not to crush the lizard in her hands. The dog skidded to a halt, spinning around to charge again. As it barreled toward her, Grace lifted the lizard and waved her hand over it, watching the green and blue creature pop into nothing. The hound slid to a stop before her and she felt its hot breath on her face. She could see the detail in the bloodred pupils, and even the whites of its eyes were stained with the color. Once more it exhaled in a loud "hmph" and readied its body to leap. Grace heard a shriek and felt herself pulled roughly aside by Rachel and Adie as the animal jumped at her.

"Jenny!" she gasped. "What are you doing?"

Again there was no answer. The hound growled in frustration and paced back and forth in front of the three girls.

"Oh my God, Grace! Get up! Run!" Rachel shouted.

"Do something, Miss!" screamed Adie.

"This is part of your lesson," said Ms. Gold, still calmly seated. "So, learn. Don't be afraid."

Grace's body was poised to leap up and break into a sprint—but still she waited for Jenny to dismiss the hound. Jenny did nothing.

A final snort signaled a charge and Grace was off, tearing across the grass. Behind her, the commotion told her that Adie and Rachel were somehow trying—and failing—to slow the massive dog. She ran along the edge of the field to the path and followed it around the back of the school. Daylight had faded, but Grace knew the hound would see well in the dark.

She could hear the hound behind her; there was no time to check if the school doors were locked. Her only options were either to take the dark country road from the school gate to the bridge, or the woods. She veered left to the woods. On the road the hound would have a straight run at her. At least in the woods there were obstacles to slow him down.

She sped under the leafy canopy, springing over fallen logs and grabbing low-lying branches to hurry her along. She ran and ran, going deeper into the woods than she'd ever been, pursued all the time by the ferocious breathing and thumping of the hound. Finally, she dared to look back, but tripped over a rock before she could catch sight of it. She landed with a grunt and felt warm ashes on her cheek.

Grace looked up and to her right. The remains of a campfire smoked and crackled. Someone was resting on their haunches, extinguishing what was left of the fire. Grace's eyes traveled upward. The boots were shadowed by a black cloak. Her throat constricted with fear. She looked straight into the ancient eyes of the Mirrorman.

His lip curled into a snarl, but, before he could move, the enormous hound lunged onto Grace's back, knocking the air out of her lungs. Hot drool dripped onto her neck, and she thought she'd be crushed beneath its weight. The hound opened its mouth to bite but suddenly paused. It had caught sight of the Mirrorman. It flattened its ears, snarled, and leaped off her and toward him.

The Mirrorman dodged the hound with ease, which angered the animal even more. It leaned back onto its hind legs and let out a low, piercing howl that rattled Grace's bones. It charged again, but the Mirrorman pulled something from beneath his coat. It looked like a silver pen but, as the man swung it forward, it stretched, like a piece of gum, and hardened into a long skinny blade. The hound couldn't stop its charge; it impaled itself on the weapon with a whimpering yelp. The old man held the massive dog in the air for a moment, then dropped it on the ground.

Grace lay panting on her stomach with her hands pressed to the ground under her shoulders. Her legs tingled with exhaustion and she knew she wouldn't outrun the Mirrorman this time. He pulled the sword from the hound's body with a grisly squelch and turned slowly toward her.

There was a sudden "whoosh" from above; Ms. Gold had landed gracefully beside Grace with a beaming smile.

"Well done, Grace," she said. "I think I underestimated—"

But as she laid eyes on the Mirrorman, Ms. Gold's mouth dropped open in horrified shock. She looked like she had been punched in the chest.

"No! No!" she gasped, backing away. "It's not possible!"

"Don't leave me, Miss!" Grace scrambled to her feet and reached for the teacher.

She heard the old man growl behind her and felt a massive impact as Ms. Gold raised her hands. A shock wave pulsed from the woman's body, distorting the air and making Grace's ears ring. She spun against the blow, using all her energy to fall in Ms. Gold's direction. Blinking against the pain in her head and keeping her hands clamped over her ears, Grace felt the teacher's arm circle her waist, and then they were soaring, soaring out of the gloom and into the night sky above.

11
the cursing of blackwood manor

Grace dropped, from a height, onto her back on the wet football field. Ms. Gold's amber eyes were panicked. The woman was shouting something at her, but Grace's ears were filled with the sound of ringing and, beneath that, a noise like an untuned radio. She shook her head, trying to communicate that she couldn't hear, but Ms. Gold gripped her shoulders and shook her.

Grace watched as Adie, Rachel, and Una tried and failed to coax the woman off her, then drag Grace away from the teacher and help her up. The ringing began to dissipate and Grace started to make out the commotion around her.

"Enough! Enough!" cried Ms. Gold, putting up her hands and signaling for the others to calm down. "I understand your concern, but this is *vitally* important!"

She approached Grace again, calmly this time, but gripped her bruised shoulders, making Grace flinch.

"Where did he come from?" Ms. Gold's voice was low, but trembled as if she was forcing herself to keep from shouting. "He shouldn't be here. Do you know where he came from?"

The woman's face was too close and her golden eyes so intense that Grace was afraid to answer. Her head ached, and her shoulders pulsed beneath the woman's fingers. Her eyes began to water. She held her breath and shook her head. The teacher searched her face for a few seconds, then let her go.

"He's dangerous," she whispered. "And he shouldn't be here."

"Who is he?" Grace breathed.

"A twisted soul," the woman replied. "He was born of malevolence and evil—he's soaked in it. If you see him again, you run. Don't speak to him, don't listen to him. You run and you don't look back. Understand?"

Ms. Gold stepped back, raising her eyes to the night sky and taking deep breaths that gradually slowed. When she lowered her face, the familiar luminosity had returned to her skin and she seemed perfectly tranquil once more.

"Go home, all of you," she said. "Stay together and stay safe. I have work to do."

The girls stood in the damp grass, watching the teacher walk briskly toward the back of the school.

"Grace?" Adie said gently, but Grace was already running at Jenny. She raised one elbow, catching Jenny in the chest and knocking her to the ground. Grace fell to her knees, grabbing handfuls of Jenny's hair and meeting her nose to nose.

"What the *hell* were you doing?" she screamed. "You tried to kill me!"

Jenny swung a fist at Grace's temple that knocked her to one side, but Grace didn't loosen her grip on Jenny's hair. They rolled and grappled on the field, screaming at each other, until Adie and Una grabbed Grace and hauled her off, while Rachel wrapped a restraining arm around Jenny's waist.

"It was part of the lesson, you moron!" Jenny shouted, her red face framed with tangled strands of hair.

"Why didn't you dismiss it?" Grace cried in reply. "You set your monster on me on purpose!"

"I was trying to control it, like Ms. Gold said. That's what we were *supposed* to do. It was *part of the lesson*."

"And part of the lesson was ripping me apart?" said Grace, still struggling against Adie and Una's grip.

"I'm *sorry*," Jenny gasped as she fought to catch her breath. "I'm sorry I couldn't control him. I was sure I could do it. I just needed more time."

"How long were you willing to wait?" said Grace. "Until he'd killed me? And why only *me*? Why did he go after me?"

"I don't know," said Jenny. "Maybe it was the lizard…and then…I don't know. Look, it was all part of the lesson."

"Stop saying that! That's not an excuse. When your monster gets out of control and tries to *eat* one of your friends, the lesson is over!"

"But it's not!" Jenny said, finally getting to her feet and pushing Rachel away. "You still don't get it. We're not kids anymore. We're witches. And witch-craft is dangerous. Our lessons will be dangerous, but we have to embrace that. What can we possibly learn if we're just doing harmless spells that achieve *nothing*? We might as well be in the lab at school. If we're going to be powerful witches, we have to learn to cope with whatever is thrown at us. We have to be able to *fight*!"

"Fight who, Jenny?" said Grace. "Don't you realize how crazy you sound?"

Jenny grasped the bronze charm around her neck—the one Ms. Gold had given her—and shook her head.

"I want to be a part of this," she said. "Body and soul. I don't want to end up a useless old woman with too many cats. I don't want to end up a boring old French teacher who makes no difference. Rhyming off the Latin names of weeds doesn't change your life. I don't want to dabble. I want to be powerful. I want to be a true witch."

"You sound just like *her*," said Grace. "Just like Ms. Gold."

Jenny rolled the charm between her finger and thumb.

"Maybe that's not a bad thing."

Grace's breath came out in bursts of mist in the cold and her eyes bored into Jenny's.

"You've changed," she whispered.

"I'm growing up," said Jenny. "And if you're all too afraid, then I guess I'm doing it alone."

She dropped the charm and turned, slowly making her way off the field.

Hot tears streaked Grace's face as the others stood still, not knowing what to do.

"She set him on me!" Grace's voice was barely audible.

Adie shook her head and wrapped her arm around her friend's shoulders.

"No way," she said. "I don't know about this

'embracing witchcraft' thing, but she's still our friend. She's still Jenny."

Grace shook her head. "She's not," she mouthed, but her friends didn't notice.

***

The red-brick building that housed the town library was comfortable and old. Inside, the single large room held lots of modern facilities, but many beautiful period features had been kept. The oak-beamed ceiling was supported by a number of black-painted pillars arranged down two sides. In the center of the room was a large octagon-shaped desk, home to the librarians and their computers. At the back of the room were four rows of partitioned desks, each holding a PC. Grace and Delilah sat in the corner, huddled in front of a flickering computer screen.

Grace had told her friends of the encounter with the Mirrorman in the woods. After all, they needed to know he was there and how dangerous he was. But what she left out of the story was her certainty that *she* had somehow brought him with her from the past. Her last flashback to the 1970s, when she was running away from him through the school, had ended with the Mirrorman actually grabbing hold of her. Grace felt she must have dragged him with her as she bounced back to her own time. This, she decided, the others didn't need to know—for now anyway. As far as Adie, Una, and Rachel were concerned, their time spell had nothing to do with the sudden appearance of the Mirrorman, so it wasn't necessary to tell Ms. Gold what they'd been up to.

"Was it a very big fight?" asked Delilah, as Grace remained focused on the screen.

"Yeah," replied Grace. "Pretty big."

"And you won't be friends again?"

Grace sighed and entered another phrase into the search engine.

"I don't know. The others don't want to break up the group, I'm sure of that. Jenny did something awful, but they don't seem to believe she did it on purpose. They'll talk to her, try to sort things out between us."

"And do you think—"

"There!" Grace said suddenly. "That's it. That's the big house the old witch burned down."

She double clicked on the image to make it full-size, and an ink sketch of the house filled the screen.

"Blackwood Manor," said Grace, reading the text beneath the image, "was built between 1738 and 1743 for Charles Hayton, one of the wealthiest commoners in Ireland at that time. The house was a striking example of the Palladian style and boasted…blah, blah, blah." She scrolled through the long description of the building's features and history.

"Following Hayton's ruination and subsequent arrest, the family abandoned the house and fled the country…blah, blah, blah… In 1839, the estate was purchased by Lord Wilbury, Baron of Millmount. Wilbury lived at Blackwood, with his young family, for only eight years before tragedy struck. The cause of the fire is unknown but, in 1847, the manor burned to the ground. Wilbury's son, Robert, is believed to have perished in the fire. Husband and wife abandoned the house after their son's death, and Blackwood was never rebuilt. Designated unsuitable for farming or raising livestock, due to the peculiarly inhospitable soil, the site remained virtually desolate until 1971, when it was donated to the local county council for the building of Saint John's Secondary School… Whoa!"

Grace leaned back and looked at Delilah.

"We've been sitting on the site of his house every day. That explains why he worked at the school, I guess."

"But it says he died in the fire," said Delilah.

"Well, *we* know what really happened," said Grace. "He was forced into being that old witch's Metamorph familiar. There's got to be more we can find."

Grace started typing again, in earnest, while Delilah's gaze drifted around the room. Finally, the small girl got to her feet and wandered between the tall bookshelves.

Nearly two hours later and Grace could feel her eyes going blurry. She rubbed at them and stretched her face in a yawn, tipping her chair back onto two legs and wriggling from side to side to ease the ache in her back. The library would be closing soon, and she hadn't found anything more on Robert Wilbury.

"I give up," she said as Delilah returned to her seat. "The Internet's useless."

Delilah smiled and dropped a large book onto the desk, open on a chapter called "The Witch of Blackwood." Grace gasped and dropped forward, her chair landing noisily back on all fours.

"Where did you get this?"

"Local History," said Delilah, grinning. "It was in the subsection on Myths and Legends."

"Delilah! You're so clever," said Grace, running her index finger down the fine text. Again, she began to read aloud.

Maureen Grogan, dubbed "The Witch of Blackwood," lived in Dunbridge sometime between 1825 and 1920. The earliest known reference to her describes Grogan as a talented healer, well-respected among the towns-people. However, later texts describe the woman definitively as a "witch." She became an outcast who plagued the more powerful citizens of Dunbridge, which culminated in the cursing of Blackwood Manor during the Famine. Like many landlords of the time, Lord Wilbury threatened his poverty-stricken tenants with violent eviction. Maureen Grogan was one such tenant. The details of the Blackwood Curse are not known, but Wilbury and his wife deserted their home after a fire in 1847. It is officially recorded that their young son died in the blaze, but rumors persisted that Grogan had captured the child and changed him into an animal; she was later seen with a large dog that answered to the boy's name.

Following Grogan's death in about 1920, there were apparent sightings of the boy, in human form, in and around the woods adjacent to the Blackwood Estate. A strange creature warped and deranged by decades of enslavement, Wilbury was said to terrorize unsuspecting hunters and fishermen that dared to enter the woods that had become his home. There were sporadic sightings of Wilbury as late as 1952, but the legend died in the latter half of the century.

Grace skimmed through the next few pages, but there was no further mention of anyone named Robert Wilbury.

"So that's it," she said. "He was freed from the curse when the witch died, but never left Blackwood. So, what, he doesn't want people on his land? A little late for that."

"Maybe he doesn't want *witches* on his land," said Delilah.

"Oh," said Grace, suddenly seeing the connection. "Grogan made him a slave and twisted his mind, but then she dies and he's set free. Free to get his revenge. You should have seen Ms. Gold's face. She was terrified of him—he must have gone after their coven in the seventies. And now…"

"And now *you* have a coven."

Grace swallowed hard.

"And I've brought him right to us."

Adie hadn't meant to spy. When she saw Grace on North Street, she had tried to catch up with her. She wanted to talk to her alone, when Jenny wasn't there and no one was angry. She had only fallen back when Delilah joined Grace at the crossroads, and they turned down Macken Street toward the library. Then curiosity had got the better of her, and she had followed them, keeping to the shadows. Maintaining a little distance, she crept through the doors after them and climbed the stairs to the library on the first floor.

The maze of bookshelves provided good camouflage as she watched the two girls set up at one of the PCs at the back of the room. They were engrossed by whatever was on the screen, but Adie couldn't make any of it out. She inched closer, darting from bookshelf to bookshelf, until she stood behind a stack, just feet from Grace and Delilah.

One quick look, she told herself, *just to see what's so interesting*. Taking a quick glance around, she stuck one foot on the second shelf from the ground and grabbed the top with her left hand. She kept climbing until she could peek over the top of the stack and catch a glimpse of the grand old house on Grace and Delilah's screen.

"Can I help you, young lady?"

Adie gasped as her feet lost their purchase on the lower shelves, her hands stayed glued to the top, and her teeth banged painfully off the shelf directly in front.

"Oww!" she said, dropping to the ground and holding a hand over her mouth.

"Is there something in particular you're looking for?" The librarian glared over her pince-nez spectacles.

"Yes," Adie replied, still holding a hand to her face. "This one."

She reached out and grabbed the first book she saw.

"*Lawnmower Maintenance and Repair*?" the librarian said.

Adie stared hard at the front cover.

"Yes," she said finally.

The librarian watched her for a moment, then pointed a long, bony finger to the desk at the center of the room.

"Check out over there," she said.

"Thanks."

Adie made her way furtively toward the main desk but, before she reached it, she saw Delilah get to her feet and walk her way. Dropping the lawnmower book on top of a pile of Harlequin romances, Adie jumped out of view and made a run for the door.

Outside, she ducked down the alleyway alongside the building and stared up at the illuminated windows on the first floor. Sighing deeply and squeezing her eyes shut, she gripped the brickwork with her fingertips and whispered a verse under her breath. A reluctant whimper escaped her mouth as her feet lifted off the ground. Using the wall for balance, she continued to rise, until she could grip the brick windowsill. Peeking over the wooden frame, she could see Delilah wandering between the bookshelves, while Grace stayed seated at the computer.

After five minutes, Adie's fingers had started cramping, and she had just decided to give up, when Delilah did something a little odd. Standing in front of a stack of books just to the right of the window, the small girl laid her palms flat against the book spines, closed her eyes, and rested her forehead on the books too. She stayed like that for nearly a minute, until there was a tremor in the stack that Adie felt through the wall, and a book shot out of a shelf farther down, falling open on the floor. Delilah slowly turned, gazed down at the book, then picked it up and headed back to Grace at the computer desks.

Adie gradually lowered herself to the ground, stretching out her aching fingers. She couldn't make sense of what she'd just seen, but she was feeling more and more uneasy about Grace's new friend.

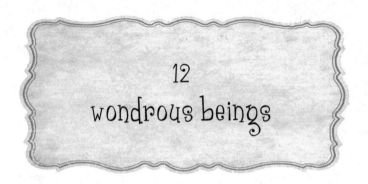

12
wondrous beings

The teenage Beth Lemon sat on the curb, just inside the school gates, watching the sun go down. She smiled as a lovely pink glow spread across the sky, giving the school grounds an otherworldly feel. She thought of the old saying,

Red sky night, shepherd's delight,
Red sky morning, shepherd's warning.

Or was it sailor's? Either way, it should be a beautiful day tomorrow. She jumped as two girls on roller skates whooshed past her, flying across the empty parking lot and squealing as they avoided colliding with each other, while doing figure eights on the pavement. A third, much smaller girl with curly pigtails crept gingerly past, stepping awkwardly on the stoppers of her roller skates and chewing on her lip.

"Get out of the way, Kitty," one of the older girls whined, as the little girl tiptoed between them. "You'll just fall in our way."

"I won't," Kitty replied earnestly, stretching her arms out.

"You can't skate," the other girl snapped, turning in a tight circle around Kitty until the smaller girl lost her balance and fell over.

Undeterred, Kitty scrambled to her feet and rolled forward at a snail's pace.

"Get lost!" the mean older girl said, giving Kitty a dig in the back that knocked her back onto the ground. Kitty sat on the pavement, her face crumpling as she began to cry. But again, even as her tears were falling, she struggled to her feet. At the edge of the parking lot, Beth tapped her fingertips on the ground, whispering soft words and staring at the little girl's roller skates.

Suddenly, Kitty was on her feet and moving forward with growing speed. Looking alarmed at first, the little girl's face broke into a huge grin as her steady feet kept her upright while her skates got faster and faster. The two older girls stopped to stare as Kitty flew over the pavement, graceful as a butterfly, twirling and spinning and whooping with delight. Beth smiled to herself. She watched the three skaters until darkness sent them home.

Vera and Meredith were late.

She wandered around the back of the school, keeping close to the wall for shelter as a cool wind picked up. As she rounded the C block, she could see the spot where she knew the anomaly to be. Staring at the flat, grassy area, she wondered how it could look so ordinary in the real world when, underneath, it was bursting with a supernatural energy that excited and terrified her.

"Return anytime," croaked a voice to her left.

Erika McGann

Beth almost screamed. Her back pressed against the wall, her fingertips gripping the cold brick. Mrs. Allan, balanced on two walking sticks, stood just a few feet away. That familiar smirk played on her mouth, but her eyes were wide and alert. Beth opened her mouth, to scream or speak, she wasn't sure, but, before she could do either, the woman was gone. Beth blinked. No one there. As she continued to stare, Meredith appeared, strolling from the woods.

"What are you doing?" she said. "I mean, what are you doing here? Aren't we supposed to meet in the parking lot?"

Beth shook her head, then nodded, then shook it again.

"I don't..." she said. "I didn't...did you see her?"

"Who?"

"Mrs. Allan."

"Mrs. Allan? Are you feeling all right?"

Beth peeled herself off the wall and steadied her shaking legs.

"I don't know."

"Hey!" They both jumped as Vera came marching around the corner. "What are you guys doing here? We were supposed to be meeting at the front gates."

Beth was about to explain that that's exactly where she had been waiting, when she realized Vera wasn't alone. A tall girl, with thick red hair almost to her waist, followed close behind. Beth recognized her. They took French together.

"What's this?" Meredith snapped.

"This," Vera replied curtly, "is Vivienne. She's heading to a party tonight in Marie Riley's house, and we're going with her. So come on, it'll be fun."

By the time they reached Marie Riley's house, the party had overflowed into the front yard. David Bowie's "Sound and Vision" blasted from the open windows, competing with the noise of the crowd that had accumulated in the driveway.

"Hey, Vera!" A handsome boy with black hair waved his hand over the throngs of people.

"Can't stop, Spud!" Vera yelled back without looking. "I'll catch you inside."

As they squeezed through the front door and into the hallway, Beth lost her grip on Meredith's shirt and was tempted to grab a lock of her blond hair rather than lose her. But instead, she was pulled apart from the other two and ended up bouncing from one side of the sitting room to the other, like a pinball, as the dancing masses got even rowdier.

After much squirming, Beth managed to free herself and escape to the kitchen at the back of the house. Finally, she caught sight of Vera's spiky red hair, but her friend was deep in conversation with Vivienne. She was holding her hand up and pointing to a ring on her middle finger. Beth couldn't make it out from where she stood, but she knew Vera wore an iron pentagram on that hand. She was probably sharing with Vivienne what it was and why she wore it. Beth felt her chest tighten and pushed her way to the back door.

She remembered how she had latched on to Vera on the very first day of school. Vera had strolled into the A block, like she owned the place, and immediately signed up for science as her first choice of subjects. Beth had followed her to that line, then to all the others, and wound up with an identical schedule. Rather than being annoyed by the follower, Vera had chatted to her with confident ease and, after discovering their mutual interest in all things paranormal, had taken her under her wing. They had been inseparable ever since.

Beth had got to know Meredith when she joined Saint John's halfway through eighth grade. She had attended the Holy Faith girls' school on the other side of town, a place with a reputation for discipline that didn't suit Meredith's rebellious character. She had been expelled in an incident that became local legend, and involved the habit of the principal, Sister Mary Catherine, a tube of superglue, and a homemade, spring-loaded device filled with thumbtacks. Her first couple of months at Saint John's began much as her days in Holy Faith had ended until, one day, she shared a lunchtime detention with Vera. Meredith had watched as the girl sketched wicked-looking symbols in her notebook, followed by lines of text in some weird language. Spying an ancient book poking out of Vera's bag, with one of the symbols on the front cover, she had stolen the book and spent several days engrossed in its contents. Vera figured out who had taken it—and came looking for her.

"Can you do some of the stuff it talks about in here?" Meredith had asked when Vera and Beth challenged her at the school gates.

"Not much," Vera had said, shrugging. "But we're learning fast."

Meredith had grinned at the two of them. "Teach me, and you can have it back."

For Beth, it had felt like a black cloud sweeping over them. She and Vera were a team, just the two of them. She didn't want a stranger in their group. But she knew Vera hadn't felt the same.

"A coven of two is not a coven," she had said many times. "A coven of three? Now that's a Wiccan number!"

Vera had returned Meredith's grin and consented; she loved a challenge.

That all seemed a long time ago now, thought Beth sadly. There were a few stragglers out the back, but she followed a pathway to the end of the garden, behind a little hedge, and, at last, found peace and quiet. She stared up at the stars, begging her tears not to fall. But the evening had been too much, and they spilled from her eyes and splashed onto the ground.

"Not your scene either, is it?"

Meredith sat in the shadow of the hedge, on an old tree stump. Shaking her head, Beth quickly wiped her eyes and sat on the ground beside her. For ten minutes, neither of them said a word. Until Meredith pointed upward suddenly.

"Shooting star. Make a wish." She looked down at Beth. "Do you wish you were at home right now?"

Beth shook her head, and Meredith nodded.

"Yeah," she said sympathetically, "I guess not. I do, though. Don't know why I came to this stupid thing. Just 'cause she said so."

Beth hugged her knees and stared at the ground.

"I hate parties," Meredith went on. "I hate being around these people. Don't you?"

"I get nervous."

"Why nervous?"

Beth shrugged.

"I don't know," she said. "I don't fit in, I suppose. I wish I could talk to people, like Vera can."

"Why?" said Meredith. "Why would you want to fit in? You're better than all these people. Think what you can do, Beth. Think about all the power you have in those tiny little hands of yours. These people are nothing."

"They're not nothing, Meredith."

Meredith sighed.

"Not nothing, that's not what I meant. I just meant… Oh, Bethany, they'll never know what we know. They'll never be able to do what we can do. We're phenomenal. We're wondrous beings!" She paused. "We hold the power of life and death in our hands."

"It comes with responsibility, though," said Beth. "You know that, right?"

"Yeah, right." Meredith smiled absently and lifted her head to gaze at the stars once more.

13
still the bully

The school bell echoed throughout the hallways as Grace pushed her way to her locker in the A block. She spied Una and Rachel in the crowd and signaled to them that she would be two minutes. Adie met her at her locker.

"Grace, do you think we should tell Ms. Lemon about the Mirrorman?"

Grace's chest tightened with worry and guilt at the mention of him.

"I don't think so," she said. "If we tell her that, we have to tell her...everything. You know, about the lessons with Ms. Gold and all that, not to mention dabbling with time spells. Best to keep it to ourselves. Besides,

Ms. Gold will probably take care of him herself and, if she couldn't, I'm sure she'd ask Ms. Lemon and Mrs. Quinlan for help."

"Yeah," said Adie, "you're probably right."

"Jenny!"

Una was waving enthusiastically up the hallway and shouting.

Grace's pace slowed, but she noticed Adie quicken her step toward the others. Una jogged up the hall to speak to Jenny, who was frowning and shaking her head as Una gripped her arm and kept talking. Grace wondered what she was saying. It certainly didn't look like Jenny was getting a talking-to.

Whatever the conversation had been about, it was rudely interrupted when Tracy Murphy appeared and pushed Una against the wall, keeping one hand on her chest and using the other to root through Una's bag. She ignored Jenny's angry protest and took a tube of lip gloss out of the backpack, promptly depositing it in her own pocket. As Adie and Rachel rushed up the hallway, Jenny pulled the lip gloss out of the

Beast's pocket and poked her in the back of the neck with it. Without missing a beat, Tracy dropped Una and fired her elbow into Jenny's shoulder. As Jenny stumbled, the Beast snatched the lip gloss out of her hand, grinned, and walked away.

"Are you guys okay?" Adie gasped as she and Rachel helped them to their feet.

"Yeah," Una said wearily.

Jenny didn't reply, but her eyes were burning with fury.

"Forget about her," Rachel said sympathetically. "You're both all right, and that's all that matters."

"Are you all right? We've got a lesson with Ms. Lemon now," Grace said, joining them. She avoided looking Jenny in the eye. The others made a move to go, but Jenny stared into the middle distance, her mouth pursed and her breathing labored.

"Are you coming, Jenny?" said Adie.

"I'm meeting with Ms. Gold," said Jenny. "I'm not bothering with Lemon and the Cat Hag anymore. They're a waste of time."

"Are you sure?" asked Adie. "I know the lessons are boring, but don't you think we need the practical *and* the theory?"

Jenny snorted, shooting Grace a sneer.

"Like I said," she answered, walking away. "Waste of time."

"Come on," said Grace, picking up Una's bag and tying it closed for her. "Ms. Lemon will be waiting."

The teacher was at the main entrance. Giving them a cheery greeting, she ushered the group outside and into the parking lot.

"No Jenny today?" she asked.

Grace was fumbling for a reply when she saw Jenny near the school gates, panting mist, with her arms rigid and her palms pressing downward. Her face was wide-eyed with surprise and delight.

"There she is," Ms. Lemon said, frowning. They watched as Jenny paced two steps forward, then back, as if not knowing which way she wanted to go. The girl seemed oblivious to them until they reached her, when her smile broadened mischievously and she shrugged her shoulders, loosening the tension in her arms.

"Jenny, are you okay?" Ms. Lemon reached out, but Jenny stepped back, still smiling.

"I'm fine," she said. "I'm better than fine."

"Oh my God!" Adie shrieked.

Grace followed her gaze to the wall, where someone was crouching, with her face and hands raised to the sky in an unnatural position. A dark red ponytail hung stiffly from the back of her head. Tracy Murphy held the awkward pose so perfectly still that she looked like a frightened mannequin. Ms. Lemon's jaw dropped as she walked toward the motionless figure with blue-lined eyes that didn't blink. The Beast was frozen solid.

"What the…?" the teacher gasped, turning to Jenny. "Did *you* do this?"

Jenny beamed and nodded. Ms. Lemon looked stricken with shock.

"Release her," she said after a long pause. "Immediately."

Jenny's smile vanished.

"I did this all by myself."

"I know you did." The teacher's voice was low and measured, like she was dealing with a dangerous animal that could lash out at any moment. "And we'll discuss it later. But for now, you *must* release her."

"Now, Beth. She hasn't done the girl any harm." Grace was startled by the sound of Ms. Gold's voice right behind her. "It's a simple immobility spell. There are no serious ramifications."

Ms. Gold stepped between the girls to stand beside Jenny and place her hand on her shoulder.

"No *ramifications*?" Ms. Lemon's voice was still carefully low. "She has cast a spell, in anger, against another child." She turned to Jenny. "This is wrong, Jenny, very wrong."

"This is a remarkable effort, Jenny," Ms. Gold said, squeezing her shoulder. "I'm very proud of you."

"Meredith!" Ms. Lemon exclaimed. "Stop this! These girls are my students and my responsibility. I won't have them exposed to your dangerous way of thinking."

"*I* have been training the girls for weeks, Beth. *I* have been honing their skills and teaching them witchcraft as it is meant to be taught."

Ms. Lemon suddenly burst forward, strands of her neat hair loosening and framing her reddening cheeks.

"How dare you!" she shouted. "You had no right to approach them. You knew very well how Vera and I felt about it, but you were your usual deceitful self. *How dare you!*"

"*They* approached *me*," said Ms. Gold calmly.

Grace felt her stomach lurch as Ms. Lemon went still.

"They asked for my help," Ms. Gold continued, "because they were frustrated, and how could they not be? They caught a glimpse of a fantastical world that they're desperate to be a part of and, instead of opening the door and guiding them in, you kept them chained outside to watch through windows. They needed someone like me."

Ms. Lemon looked to each of the girls, but none of them could meet her eyes. Grace glanced up only long enough to see the hurt etched across the teacher's face.

"It's not too late, Beth," said Ms. Gold, her voice still smooth as honey. "We could work together."

Ms. Lemon's eyes went wide.

"Are you crazy?" she breathed. "You're dangerous and irresponsible! You'll destroy the good nature that these girls have. Look what you've done already!" She pointed to the motionless Tracy.

"Very well, then," said Ms. Gold. "It's obvious we can't work in tandem, so we'll let them choose. The girls will choose with whom they wish to continue their training, and the other will back off. Sound fair?"

Ms. Lemon's pained look worsened as she glanced at the girls, all with their eyes averted.

"Girls," said Ms. Gold. "If you wish to resume theoretical lessons with Ms. Lemon, then please feel free to leave with her now. Otherwise, stay with me and continue on the extraordinary journey you have begun."

Grace looked at the others, her eyes begging

someone to speak. But nobody looked up. Adie and Rachel stared fixedly at their shoes, while Una twisted her thumb and finger in a hole in the sleeve of her sweater. Grace took a breath, but before she could speak, Ms. Lemon leaped forward, meeting Ms. Gold face-to-face.

"Why did you come back here?" she said. "What do you want?"

"This is my home," Ms. Gold replied. "You chased me out once before. You won't do it again."

There was a long pause before Ms. Lemon stepped back, looking frazzled in a way Grace had never seen before. She gave the girls a reproachful look and marched back to the school.

"That was unpleasant," said Ms. Gold, still gripping Jenny's shoulder. "I apologize. But now I'm free to take you all firmly on the road to Wicca. First things first, let's unfreeze this poor girl before anyone else sees her. Jenny, will you do the honors?"

Jenny grinned happily as Grace turned to catch a last glimpse of Ms. Lemon. But she was already gone.

14
back in time

The heady air of Mr. Pamuk's shop was oddly relaxing, and Grace took her time wandering around the place. She hadn't intended to stick around for Ms. Gold's lesson anyway, but at the first mention of the Mirrorman, she had made her excuses and left.

She wondered now what new spell the others were learning, but she was afraid her face would have betrayed the guilt she felt at bringing him into their world. Ms. Gold had said they needed to capture him, to bind his powers and protect themselves, but Grace knew what she needed was to send him back to his own time.

"Is there anything in particular you are searching for?" Mr. Pamuk's smile was as welcoming as ever.

"Figwort," Grace said firmly. "Green Figwort."

Mr. Pamuk's eyebrows lifted almost to his hairline.

"Rare indeed," he said. "Did you know that the plant grows in this country?"

"I know," Grace replied. "There was a little patch of it near here, but it's…it's used up."

"I see." His eyes searched her face with interest. "You know, when one must harvest a specimen that is close to extinction, it is advisable to use as little as possible. And always to leave enough for the plant to rejuvenate."

Grace felt her face grow hot.

"Oh," she said. "I didn't realize. I'll be careful in the future."

"It is not in the seller's best interests," said the shopkeeper, "to pry into the business of his clients. Though Green Figwort is scarce, it is fortunately not a frequent ingredient in Wiccan recipes." He examined her closely again, but with his smile still wide and caring. "One hopes one's clients remain as safe as possible."

Grace smiled shyly and nodded her head in understanding.

"Otherwise," he said, with a sudden laugh, "I might run out of customers!"

Grace watched him duck under the hanging partition behind his desk and heard him rummage through boxes and stacks of jars. As she waited, she walked slowly around the cavern, drawn to the enchanted mirror that had first shown her the Mirrorman. A familiar feeling of dread filled her body as her fingers traced the gilded frame that she had seen, most recently, in her nightmares.

She fixed on her reflection in the glass. Like before, the image deepened until she felt she might reach out and feel her own cheek. Her head became light as the whisper of mist began curling in the center of the frame. Still she did not move.

"An enchanted looking glass is still just a looking glass...just a reflection." Mr. Pamuk's words echoed in her mind, and she steeled her courage, refusing to back away. Even when the face formed, and the eyes flickered open—one blue, one milky white—she didn't look away. Holding her breath, she waited for his useless attack.

But the face didn't lunge at her. The eyes closed and the face dropped back, like a pebble in a lake, leaving ripples that traveled to the edges of the mirror. The ripples gradually resolved to reveal a blurry scene, which jarred like stop-motion animation, randomly shot through with bursts of black and purple. Grace leaned in and could just make out the P block, the site of the demon well.

There were flying limbs and moving bodies passing through the image, accompanied by distorted, panicky sounds. It was some kind of emergency. Through the turmoil she suddenly recognized Adie's dark curls and almond-shaped eyes. Then Rachel's fair face. Both were on their knees, with their hands bound, scream-ing. As she caught her breath, there was a glimpse of Una opposite them, her short black hair hanging down as she cried in anguish. There was a shot of Jenny's panicked eyes, then the image swung from left to right, and the figures blurred and started to fade.

Grace smacked her hands onto the glass, trying to draw the image back so she could see more. But it drifted into the mist, and soon she found herself staring into her own reflection. She sank to her knees and dug her phone out of her bag, scrolling furiously through her contacts.

"Adie?"

"Hey, Grace, what's up? You didn't stick around for the lesson." Adie's voice was calm and normal.

Grace took a few breaths, relief bringing tears to her eyes.

"Are you okay?" Adie went on. "I know you're upset about Ms. Lemon. We all are... It's just—"

"It's okay," Grace breathed, climbing to her feet. "I'm okay. Just checking in. I'll call you later."

She leaned her back against the mirror, taking long deep breaths.

"Green Figwort," Mr. Pamuk declared, emerging

from behind the partition with a large jar in his hands. "I must warn you, though, it's not cheap."

Grace rooted for the cash in her pocket—all the money she had in the world—and held it out to him.

"I'll take it," she said.

***

At lunchtime the next day, Grace hunkered down in one corner of the deserted P block, just feet from where she knew the demon well to be. The silver fork squeaked against the porcelain dish; she steadied herself and placed her hand on the yearbook that lay beside her. She held it open on the photograph of the young Mrs. Quinlan, Ms. Lemon, and Ms. Gold, focusing on their faces. The first time spell had stopped bouncing Grace back to 1977. But now she needed to restart it. She chanted softly:

"Beloved Chronos, lord of time,
Thy bounty and thy strength divine,

With meek and humble force I cast
This charm to view what now is past."

She held her concentration as the metallic clanging picked up speed and settled into a rhythm.

Clickety-click-click.

Clickety-click-click.

Grace let the sound wash over her, closing her eyes against the flashing light and the foghorn blast. She felt a cool breeze brush through her hair.

She opened her eyes to find herself standing on the grassy patch where the P block didn't yet exist. It was lunchtime in the old Saint John's, and the school thronged with students opening and closing lockers and sitting cross-legged in groups on the floor. Grace hurried down the hallway and turned left, hoping that the coven's use of the library had not been a onetime thing. Looking through the square pane of glass in the door, she could see a few people scattered throughout the large room. She was in luck, for tucked in one corner, barely visible behind a high stack of shelves, were Vera, Beth, and Meredith.

They were arguing again. Meredith stood with her arms outstretched, talking fast with her face pinched in frustration. Vera was perched on a table, with one foot on a chair, a vision of calm indifference. She appeared to be listening impassively while Meredith gestured and stamped her foot, finally crossing her arms and pursing her lips. A few seconds of frozen silence then appeared to pass between the three, until Vera swung her foot off the chair and stood.

Grace couldn't hear what she said, but whatever it was sent an angry flush through Meredith's cheeks and, as Vera walked past her, Grace was sure the young Ms. Gold's shaking fists would strike out. But the girl just stood and glared at Beth, as if expecting some reaction. There was none, so Meredith stalked away through the exit in the far corner. Beth sat alone with her head bowed and her long bangs shading one eye. This was Grace's chance.

Taking a quick look around to make sure she was alone, she held out her hands and whispered under her breath. It took three attempts to catch the Glamour buzz but, finally, she was able to look at her reflection in the window and see a stranger looking back. Grace was now shorter, with sandy-colored hair, a squarer chin, and blue eyes instead of green. It was nothing compared to Rachel's skill, but it would do. She pushed through the door.

"Hi. It's Bethany, isn't it?" Grace spoke quietly, but there was little chance of anyone in the library overhearing them.

Beth shook her bangs to one side and looked up with shy, hazel eyes.

"Beth," she said warily.

"Beth, right. I'm Gray…Anna. Grayanna."

Beth frowned.

"It's French," said Grace. "My, uh, mom's French. From France. She doesn't live there anymore. She lives here, obviously. 'Cause I live here…obviously… Anyway, it's a French name."

Grace resisted the urge to kick herself, but Beth just smiled.

"I like it," she said.

"Thanks."

Grace took a seat and willed herself to calm down.

"Look," she said, "I hate to get straight to it, but I don't know how long I have here and I need your help."

The hazel eyes frowned again.

"I know we've never met before, but I know a lot about you. Much more than just your name. And I know about your friends as well—Vera and Meredith. I know that you're"—Grace leaned forward—"*witches*."

Beth started and looked around, panicked, though there was no one close enough to hear. She looked back at Grace, her breathing quick and her eyes round with worry. She grabbed her bag and jumped to her feet.

"Wait!" said Grace, catching her arm and holding it. "I'm not going to hurt you, or expose you, or anything like that. I just need your help."

"Have you been spying on us?" Beth hissed.

"Not exactly," replied Grace. "But I did come here to find you. You see, *I'm* a witch too."

She had never said as much before and felt an odd swell of pride declaring it out loud.

"I don't believe you," said Beth.

"I'll prove it."

Grace looked around for a life template. She focused her attention downward, hoping the wooden desk would be enough to work with, and whispered, "*Ex vita vetera, vita nova.*"

In her mind's eye, she wrapped a sphere around the life template, copying it, and pulling it to her open hand. She pictured the sphere opening, and in the center of her palm appeared a small, yellow frog. Beth's mouth fell open. She gazed at the animal with growing delight and lifted a finger to touch the creature's back.

"*Ribbit,*" it croaked.

She giggled, raising her hand to touch it again. The frog made tiny clicking sounds as she stroked its back.

"You *are* a witch," she whispered.

Grace exhaled in relief, not realizing she'd been holding her breath.

"So what do you need from us?" Beth asked.

"This is going to sound really strange, but I'm not from your time. I'm from the future."

Beth's smile disappeared as she gently picked up the frog and held it to her chest, though Grace saw her steal a glance at the school crest on Grace's sweater that was missing from her own.

"I've been here before," Grace went on. "My friends and I did this spell, and it…well, it didn't work properly. Anyway, I brought something back with me to my own time. Not something, *someone*. He shouldn't be there and I need to bring him back here. But I don't know how."

"Can't your friends help you?"

"They don't know it was me who brought him to our time and we're…we're not getting along very well at the moment. It's complicated."

Beth tickled the frog under the chin.

"I see."

"Will you help me?"

Beth softly blew through her lips, then gasped as the frog suddenly leaped out of her hands and onto the bookcase. She chased after it, unable to reach the top shelf, and let out a helpless cry as the animal sprang off the end of the bookcase. Before it hit the ground, Grace flicked her fingers in the air and the companion popped into nothing. The light popping sound was followed by the faraway sound of a train.

"Oh God," said Grace, "I'm about to bounce back to my own time. Hurry, please tell me you'll help."

Beth was waving her hands in the space where the frog used to be.

"Beth!" said Grace. "I need to know if you'll help me. *Please.*"

Clickety-click-click.

Clickety-click-click.

"I'll talk to the others," replied Beth. "When will you be back?"

"I don't know," Grace said. "I can't control it. Please promise you'll talk to them soon. As soon as possible."

Clickety-click-click.

Clickety-click-click.

"What happens?" said Beth. "Will you just disappear?"

"Promise, Beth. *Promise me!*"

Beth's face illuminated in a flash, and beneath the

foghorn blast, Grace could just make out the words she was mouthing.

"I promise."

15
a witch from the future

After the surprising events in the library, Beth left, hugging her books and walking with her head down. Her satchel hung over one shoulder, but she liked the comfort of having something to hold in front of her body as she walked the hallways alone. Even now, as a senior, she felt intimidated by other students, especially those in groups.

She gave herself a mental shake and tried to focus on what to do about the girl in the library. She caught up with Vera as their chemistry class filed into the lab. They took the desk at the back on the left-hand side, the one farthest from the teacher's desk.

"Hey, V, did ya check out that new band, The Clash? They're slammin', huh?" A boy with a short Mohawk stood awkwardly in front of their desk, his hands shoved into his pockets as he swayed from side to side. Beth blushed for him as he faked a bored look around the room.

"Yeah," replied Vera.

The boy nodded as if she had given a long and interesting critique.

"Yeah," he said, still nodding. "Did you get their new record?"

"Yeah."

"'Cause I can record it for you, if you didn't get it."

"Got it."

"Right, right," the boy replied, filling the silence with more nodding. "Yeah, so anyway…see ya later."

"See ya."

Beth smiled as Vera unpacked her bag, oblivious. Boys always hung around Vera, but she never paid attention to them. Maybe they hung around her *because* she never paid attention to them. They were always asking her opinion on the latest band or the latest movie, or even trying to sneak a compliment from her on their latest hairdo. The girls thought she was cool too and, inevitably, if Vera dyed her hair or came to school with a new piercing, a dozen girls would copy it within the week. Vera was so cool, she didn't even know she was cool. She didn't care—and that made her the coolest girl in school.

"I met someone in the library today," said Beth as she dragged a high stool across the floor and sat down.

"Really?" said Vera with interest. "That nerdy fella who stares at you in English, by any chance?"

Beth's face flushed and she shook her head.

"No, no. A girl." She paused. "Another *witch*."

Vera stared at her with narrowed eyes. Beth wondered if she was thinking of Vivienne.

"*What* other witch?"

"She says she's from the future. From *this* school. Has our school crest on her sweater and everything," said Beth. "I guess they add that to the uniform."

"Did she pull the other one?" Vera asked, opening

her notebook as the teacher began scribbling with white chalk on the blackboard.

"Pull the other what?"

"*Leg*, my dear Bethany. She's pulling your leg. You know, your gullibility is one of the reasons I love you."

"She *proved* it," Beth replied. She pretended to ignore the reaction that got from Vera and got started on her chemistry notes. She felt Vera's eyes boring into her, until the girl grunted impatiently.

"Go on, then," she said. "You have my full attention. How did she prove it?"

"Originated a little frog, then and there, on her first try."

"Hmm," said Vera, nodding. "Not bad."

"She's young too," Beth continued. "Only about fourteen, I'd say. She asked for our help. Apparently she brought someone back to her time by accident. She needs to return him to our time, but she doesn't know how."

"Brought back who?"

"She didn't say. What do you think? Should we help?"

"I'll think about it," replied Vera.

"We'll need Meredith. She's good at sourcing spells."

When Vera didn't answer, Beth said gently, "Are you two going to work this out?"

"Meredith's getting too big for her boots," said Vera. "I don't want her knowing there's another witch around while we're still working on the anomaly. Let's keep this to ourselves for now."

That night, under the moonless sky, Beth stood shivering against the cold, holding her coat collar closed over her neck. She could just make out Vera's spiky-haired silhouette near the entrance of the C block and the glowing butt of her cigarette as she put it out against the wall. Beth shook her head. She hated the smell of cigarette smoke, and Vera reeked of it.

Turning away, she gazed into the blackness of the woods, listening to the eerie whistling of the wind as it blew through the trees. Meredith had once told her the woods were haunted. She had scoffed at the idea, but every time they came out to this place she felt a shiver up her spine that was more than just the cold and wind. The feeling had grown after they came across the anomaly. They had studied it, watched it, taken aura readings from its edge, and all they knew was that it was fit to burst with magical force, as if the tiniest pinprick would cause it to explode into the world, expelling whatever it held in a supernatural fireworks display.

As she watched the woods, Beth could imagine herself lost in there—it was so black and so dense. She wondered if there really was a ghost, the trapped spirit of someone who had wandered into the trees and never found their way out. She felt the shiver again. Then something else. The creep of cold fingers along her cheek. She jumped and screamed.

"Every time," said Meredith, laughing. "You're so easy."

"Don't *do* that!" Beth said, backing off and pulling her collar tight again. "Don't sneak up like that."

"Thinking about the ghost in the woods? You know, Mrs. Allan says it's a boy who was imprisoned by a witch in the woods, and now he can never leave.

Imagine that. Being trapped in there forever, tormented and alone."

Beth turned away to walk toward the anomaly, and Meredith snuck up a hand to touch the back of her neck.

"Stop!" Beth squealed again as Meredith dissolved into more giggles.

"There's no such thing as a ghost in the woods," Vera said flatly as she joined them by the anomaly.

"How do *you* know?" asked Meredith, her tone suddenly gone cold.

Vera ignored the question, pulling several skinny candles from her pocket and pushing them into the ground, forming a circle. She lit each one in turn.

"Take your places," she said finally.

"This is a waste of time," said Meredith. "So what if the energy pattern here differs from our world? What will that tell us? It's obviously a portal to something; we know that. All we have to do is look inside."

"Stop being a child, Meredith, and take your place," replied Vera.

Meredith stared at her in silence.

"Meredith," said Beth gently, "it's safer to work it out this way, if we can. We don't know what's on the other side. It could be dangerous."

"We can handle it," said Meredith, still holding Vera's gaze.

"Enough," said Vera, waving her hand dismissively. "Just do what you're told."

Meredith stared at her again, her jaw grinding from side to side. After a few moments her face lifted.

"Fine," she said, settling herself at one side of the circle with her legs crossed.

Beth pulled a small shaker from her coat pocket and sprinkled the contents between the candles. When the shaker was empty, Vera grabbed handfuls of grass, wrenching it from the ground and tossing it all over the circle.

"Hands out," she said. "Concentrate."

She and Beth held their arms out, palms down, and closed their eyes. Beth could feel the heat from the candle in front, almost close enough to burn her. In the quiet, she heard a shuffling to her left. Sneaking a look with one eye, she saw Meredith pull something from her satchel and roll it into the circle. Vera's eyes snapped open as the object hit her boot and stopped. A cool breeze swept over them as Beth realized what lay at Vera's feet.

"A crystal ball?" said Beth, as Vera leaned in for a closer look. "Vera! Don't go near it!"

As she spoke, a wisp of black mist shot from the ground, forming a clawed hand, and grabbed Vera by the neck. As she began to choke, the black claws sank into her skin, not drawing blood, but disappearing into her. Beth watched in horror as a second arm formed in the mist, the hand gripping Vera's face and pushing into her flesh. Vera gasped against the onslaught and her eyes began to glow an unnatural shade of violet.

In her shock, Beth barely registered the whoosh of movement beside her as Meredith leaped forward, kicking the crystal ball as far as she could, dropping a porcelain cup on the ground, and smashing it with her foot. Something in the cup sublimated into smoke, and Meredith jumped on Vera's back, holding her over the smoke and hissing the words, "*Exitus, exitus, exitus.*"

Vera shook her head, refusing to breathe in the smoke, until Meredith grabbed a handful of her spiky hair and pulled sharply. Finally, Vera sucked in a breath, and the neon violet of her eyes faded. Meredith sank to one side, shaking with the rush of adrenaline in her system, and smiled broadly.

"It *is*," she said, panting. "It's a demon well!"

Seconds later Vera had Meredith on the ground, her hands around her throat.

"You rat!" she screamed. "You filthy rat! How dare you? I could destroy you! I could finish you off right here."

Meredith struggled against the viselike grip on her neck.

"I..." The words were choked in her throat. "I knew what I was doing! I...I had it all worked out!"

"Vera!" Beth gasped as Meredith's eyes rolled back in her head. "Let go!"

Vera only leaned harder onto her hands, pushing her face right up to Meredith's.

"You think you're better than me?" she hissed. "You think you're stronger? If it weren't for me, you'd still be pulling childish pranks and bouncing from school to school. Without me, you're *nothing*! I run this coven. It's *mine*!"

Meredith was losing consciousness, her hands scrabbling ever more weakly at Vera's shoulders.

"Vera!" Tears streamed down Beth's face as she begged. "Please stop! You're killing her! *Please!*"

Vera ignored her. Beth saw the change of color in Meredith's face and the light fading from her eyes. Springing behind them, she looped her arms around Vera's and pulled as hard as she could.

"Stop it! That's enough! Stop it!"

Vera, startled, loosened her arms, letting herself and Beth tumble backward. Beth heard the sound of Meredith coughing, followed by a loud gasp as she sucked the air back into her lungs. She crawled over to the gasping girl, instinctively stroking the golden blond hair and saying soothing words. But Meredith pushed Beth's hands away and struggled unsteadily to her feet, her face red and her eyes watering. She turned to Vera, who was glaring at her with fury.

"I knew what it was." The words sounded painful coming from Meredith's bruised throat. "I knew what to do. But you wouldn't listen to me. You *never* listen to me!"

Vera didn't answer but held her icy stare.

"I had it all prepared," Meredith went on. "You were safe. I would have kept you safe, no matter what happened. You're like sisters to me, both of you. I would never have let you come to harm."

Vera walked slowly forward until she stood right in front of Meredith's shaking frame.

"Well, *sister*," she whispered. "Your time in this coven is over. Walk away…and don't look back."

She stepped back and gripped Beth's shoulder. Meredith's face crumpled. The blond girl stood there for a moment, her face streaked with tears, before Vera dismissed her with a lift of her chin. Beth watched Meredith's unsteady exit through the back gates and leaned against the support of Vera's hand as she stifled a sob.

"It'll be all right," Vera whispered. "There's a replacement—we'll still have a third. I've taken care of it."

But Vivienne would be no replacement for Meredith, and Vera's unsteady voice told Beth that, deep down, she knew it too. Their family was broken. It was all over.

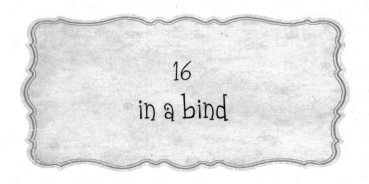

16
in a bind

Still in the guise of "Grayanna," Grace sat in the library, nervously twisting a strand of short, sandy hair around her fingers, avoiding the young Vera's gaze. She'd gone back specifically to ask for her help, and now she was wondering how the teenager could already have the same terrifying presence that she would have later, as a middle-aged woman. Her pale eyes were unblinking, and Grace began to sweat like she was in the interrogation room of a police station. Self-consciously, she rubbed at her chin, but carefully, so as not to inadvertently shake off any of the Glamour spell. If her appearance suddenly changed into the Grace that Vera

Quinlan tutored, she feared the consequences in her own time.

"So you're *Grayanna*. From the future," Vera said.

"Um-hm." Grace cleared the frog in her throat. "Yes, I am."

"And who exactly have you pulled from our time to yours?"

Grace had considered lying about this—not knowing if Vera's coven had yet encountered the Mirrorman for what he really was—but they'd find out eventually, so she went with the truth. Kind of.

"The groundskeeper here."

"Creepy Bob?" said Beth. She and Vera exchanged a look of surprise.

"Hmm," Vera murmured. "He's no great loss to us, but I suppose we don't want to mess up the time line. No more than you already have, that is."

Grace gulped.

"We've found a spell that could work," said Vera, "and we'll help you perform it. But we're missing a vital piece of equipment, and we can't get hold of one here."

She unfolded a yellowing sheet of paper and smoothed it out on the desk, displaying a detailed sketch of what looked like a slingshot without the sling.

"It's a Balau Dowser," she said. "They're difficult to get, and sourcing one will cost a fortune."

"I've seen one of these before," Grace said excitedly, recognizing it from the awful scavenger hunt in Mrs. Quinlan's attic. "In your—um, it's in the attic of a house in my time."

"Good. Then you can get it."

"Can I?" Grace suddenly very much regretted mentioning it. "I don't know. It belongs to this crabby old witch, and there's no way I can ask her for it, even to borrow."

"So don't ask for it. Just take it."

"You mean steal it? I couldn't!" Grace exclaimed. "She'll find out and go mental."

"Don't be so chicken," said Vera. "Just sneak in and grab it. You scared of some little old lady?"

The irony of the young Mrs. Quinlan unwittingly speaking of herself like this made Grace pause for a moment.

"We can't do the casting without it," said Beth.

"All right," replied Grace. "I'll do my best."

"And we need something of Creepy Bob's. Something personal," said Vera.

Grace wasn't going to budge on this one.

"No, I can't get you that. I...I don't even know where he is."

"Hey, Squirt, we're not doing this for ourselves. We're being nice and helping you out, remember? So how about a little cooperation?"

"I would," Grace stammered, "but I really don't know where he is. I wouldn't know where to start looking."

Vera emitted something close to a growl and shook her head.

"Then the casting's off. It won't work if we can't pinpoint his energy."

"Wait," said Grace. "I might know where he lives in *this* time. It's out in the woods. If we can find where he camps out, there's bound to be something there we can use."

Grace tried to look as confident as possible, hoping

that she would be able to find the spot where Jenny's hound had pounced on her in her own time, near the Mirrorman's camp. He'd remained in and around the woods all his life—he was a creature of habit. With luck, Grace could lead them to his permanent dwelling among the trees.

Grace stood. "Let's go."

The woods were filled with flitting shadows and creaking branches straining against the wind. Grace could hear Vera's breath behind her, labored and somehow threatening. There was a constant air of suspicion about her, and Grace felt under pressure to locate the Mirrorman's camp as quickly as possible. However, the farther they went into the dense woodland, the less sure she became of her whereabouts. After nearly an hour's trekking, Vera gripped her arm roughly.

"Where are you taking us, Grayanna? We've been walking for ages."

"It's around here somewhere," Grace replied. "I'm sure we're really close."

Vera's grip tightened. In the dark, her spiky hair made an eerie silhouette.

"If this is some sort of setup," she warned, her breath close. "If you've been playing us—"

"It's here!" Beth said suddenly, to Grace's great relief. "It's just over there. Do you see it?"

She pointed to the outline of a dome, just yards ahead.

The Mirrorman's home was a small circular wall of crumbling stone covered with an intricate domed roof of woven branches. A few feet from the hut's entrance were the scorched remains of a campfire, ringed with large pebbles. A black pot hung from a wrought-iron stand over the ashes, and a hand-made fishing rod rested on a three-legged stool nearby. It seemed an unlikely domestic situation for a Wiccan legend that terrified hunters and chased fishermen from the woods. Grace couldn't help feeling a small pang of pity for such a lonely and meager existence.

"There's sod all inside," said Vera, the flame of her lighter glowing through the woven roof as she poked her head inside the hut. "How does this guy live with *nothing*?"

"Guess we could take the pot or the fishing rod," replied Beth. "They're a bit big, though. Awkward."

"We could just take the fishing fly," said Grace, lifting the fishing rod and handling it with interest.

"The what?" said Vera.

Grace pulled on the line of the fishing rod, lifting the lure that hung on the end to eye level. It was strange. Everything the Mirrorman owned was minimal and functional, ugly and fit for one purpose only—but the lure on his fishing rod was something else. It was an object of beauty. The main feather came from no bird she knew of—its silver and purple edge almost glowing, though there was no light in the woods. And in the head of the fly was a tiny jewel, like a sparkling eye. Grace twisted the line in her fingertips, and the fly spun slowly, showing off its stunning colors and delicate design. The hut, the stool, and the fishing rod were not made by magic, but the fly looked too extraordinary to be anything other than magical. She detached the lure from the line with a sharp *snap*.

"We'll take this," she said.

"Hold on," said Vera, flicking on her lighter again and peering at something shiny sticking from the ground by the wall of the hut. "What's this?"

Puzzled, Grace and Beth looked at the metal object that seemed to be out of place in its surroundings. It was a polished brass ornament, partially buried in the soil. Using her lighter to illuminate the object, Vera dug her fingers around it and pulled it free. She froze. It was a figure, with hands bound behind his back and sticks of brass piercing his head and body.

"Vera, drop it!" Beth screamed, but it was too late.

Vera's whole body spasmed and she collapsed to the ground, still gripping the brass figure in her right hand. Beth raced forward, trying to pry the ornament from her fingers, but it was no use. Vera lay unconscious, her eyes open and rolling back in her head, her arm jerking occasionally, as if the figure was sending shocks through her system.

"Vera!" Beth yelled, gripping her shoulders and shaking her. "Vera, wake up!"

Vera's head lolled from side to side as Beth continued to shake her in a panic. Grace pulled her away.

"Stop it," she said. "You'll hurt her."

Beth leaned against her and sobbed uncontrollably.

"What *is* that thing?" Grace whispered.

"A Muerte figurine," Beth said through shaky breaths. "A binding ornament. Creepy Bob must have left it here to protect his home."

"What's it doing to Vera? Is she alive?"

"Yes, but barely. They're so powerful they can bind your powers, your mind for...*forever*."

"How do we undo it?" said Grace.

"We can't," wept Beth. "It would take an extremely powerful Wiccan to break a binding like this—there's no witch with that kind of force around here. The caster himself would have to break the spell."

Grace looked mournfully at Vera's twitching body, so horrible in the dark with her flat, unseeing eyes. The Mirrorman hunted witches on his land,

and this one had invaded his actual home. There was no way he would release the binding. This was all Grace's fault.

As loud drops of rain began to fall, they half-carried, half-dragged Vera's body inside the hut. They would never be able to carry her out of the woods alone. As they laid her on a flattened bed of dried leaves and ferns, Beth brushed spikes of dyed red hair off Vera's forehead.

"Do you think it's safe to—"

"*Shhh,*" said Grace suddenly, lowering her voice to a whisper. "Did you hear that?"

Beth cocked her head to listen. There was a rustling outside. Something was moving through the undergrowth.

"Could be a rat?" Beth whispered. "Or a rabbit?"

"Too big," said Grace, reaching up and quietly working a switch free from the woven roof.

She stepped toward the doorway, ready to whack whatever it was with the slender branch. The rustling got closer. It was almost to the doorway. Grace braced herself.

"Aaahhh!" she screamed, leaping outside and swiping left and right with the switch.

"Stop!" someone yelled as they fell to the ground, covering their head with their arms. "Stop it!"

Grace froze, mid-swat, and gazed down at the girl lying in the weeds, with her golden hair tangled around her slender arms.

"*Meredith?*"

Meredith peeked out from under her elbow.

"Who are you?"

"Meredith!" Beth gasped, running from the hut and dropping to her knees to hug her. "What are you doing here?"

Meredith looked between Beth and Grace for a moment, then glanced quickly toward the hut.

"I followed you here," she said. "Where's Vera?"

"Inside," replied Grace, leading the way.

Beth's tears fell afresh as she took Meredith's hand and followed Grace into the hut. Meredith started when she saw the pale, twitching figure on the ground. Her eyes went to the figurine still clenched in Vera's hand, and the blood drained from her face.

"That's not—" she stopped mid-sentence.

"A Muerte figurine," Beth said, nodding. "We didn't see it before she picked it up." She lunged forward and gripped the front of Meredith's shirt. "You have to help us. *Please*. I'm so sorry about everything. I didn't want it this way. Please don't leave us alone!"

Meredith seemed unable to take her eyes from the shuddering body on the ground. Each twitch was mirrored by a flinch in her own face. Her lip curled as she watched.

"Only the caster can break this spell," she said. "Or a Wiccan virtuoso. Do you know of either?"

"The caster is in my time, in the future," said Grace. "Beth and Vera promised to help me bring him back here."

Meredith stared at her with a dubious smile.

"The *future*?"

"It's true," said Beth. "Creepy Bob followed her to

the future. This is his place—we came here to find something of his for a casting."

There was a pregnant pause.

"You kept all this from me?"

"Not all of it," Beth stammered. "We had no idea about Creepy Bob. And all the future stuff, well, Vera felt..."

"Vera had already decided it was time to start cutting me out of the picture," Meredith said coolly.

"No! No, it wasn't like that!"

"Then tell me, Beth. What was it like?"

Beth faltered under Meredith's intense gaze. Her eyes watered again, and her voice became nothing more than a whisper.

"Please help us bring Bob back here, Meredith. He's the only one who can save Vera. *Please.*"

Grace watched the golden-haired girl as the faraway sound of a train began to build. Meredith let the silence go on for what felt like forever.

Come on, Grace thought, *say yes. Beth can't handle this alone.*

As the metallic crescendo swamped Grace's ears, a self-satisfied smile spread across Meredith's face.

"All right," she said, "I'll help you."

Grace heaved a sigh of relief as light swelled around her.

"But I'm back in the coven," said Meredith. "And from now on, we're gonna do things my way."

And that was the last thing Grace heard before a foghorn blast sent her crashing into the future, leaving Beth, Meredith, and an unconscious Vera far behind her.

17
b and e in wilton place

Grace had sunk exhausted into bed that night, yet found sleep elusive—and when it did come, it was filled with dreams and visions. She was standing at the doorway of the Mirrorman's hut. Meredith was leaning against the trunk of a tree, watching her, in a shaft of sunlight that made her blond hair shimmer. Grace knew she was dreaming, yet could feel the cool breeze on her bare arms and the crunchy woodland floor under her shoes. She stepped inside the hut and saw Beth, with her back to the door, sitting by Vera's motionless body. Vera still clutched the Muerte doll in one hand, but she was awake. She stared at Grace with terrified eyes.

"She's awake, Beth," said Grace.

Beth turned around slowly to look at Grace—but it wasn't her at all. Delilah's brown eyes stared back at her. She smiled, fingering a bronze charm around her neck—the one Ms. Gold had given to Jenny.

"No!" Vera whispered, as Delilah pulled a dagger from nowhere and plunged it into her heart.

Grace staggered backward out of the hut, screaming. Outside, it was pitch-black and the wind was howling. The undergrowth clutched at her ankles, and she fell, landing on grass at the site of the demon well. She gasped, feeling something sharp under her hand. It was the Mirrorman's fishing fly. She held it up to the moonlight and its jeweled eye sparkled.

"That doesn't belong to you." Meredith was just a few feet away. "It's his."

She pointed to the site of the well, where the ground swelled as something pushed from beneath. The grass and soil turned over, and a white hand burst through, followed by another. Grace scrambled backward as the Mirrorman's head and shoulders emerged, hunching as he dragged the rest of his body from the earth. He reached for the fly in her hands, and Grace felt the feathers flutter against her fingers. Suddenly, a net was flung over him; he curled up in a ball and was dragged back to the hole. He made horrible gurgling cries as Meredith, with an airy wave of her hand, rolled him along the ground. She smirked at Grace, as she pushed him back down, down into the demon well.

Grace looked at the fly in her hands. Its feathers fluttered as if in response to the Mirrorman's desperate screams. When the screaming stopped, the fly lay still and its sparkling eye dulled to black. Meredith's laugh made her look up just as the net engulfed her.

Grace struggled herself awake.

Her sheet was drenched with sweat and her duvet was halfway across the room. She dragged it back onto the bed and curled up, pulling it over her head. Her heart was still pumping too fast, and she took long, deep breaths to help her drift back into an uneasy sleep.

At half past midnight, her phone's alarm buzzed her awake.

***

Half an hour later, under cover of darkness, Grace and Delilah tiptoed across Wilton Place and around the back of Mrs. Quinlan's house. Grace had never snuck out of her house before, and her palms had been sweaty since she left her bedroom—if this was what being rebellious felt like, she would much rather stay a Goody Two-shoes.

Despite Delilah's gory role in Grace's dream— which Grace couldn't face telling her about—she was grateful for her company as the two girls passed into the shadow of the ramshackle building. Delilah hadn't hesitated when Grace asked her to help retrieve something from Old Cat Lady's attic, using a breaking and entering spell. For such a timid girl, Delilah didn't seem afraid of much. Perhaps that's why she'd been in the horrible dream in the first place.

"Remember," said Grace, pulling a damp coil of ribbon from her pocket, "the cats are everywhere, so watch where you put your feet. Are you sure you want to do this?"

The small girl nodded.

Grace wrapped the ribbon around the handle of the back door, tying a double knot.

"Open Sesame," she said softly.

There was a click, a short creak, and the door swung open.

"Seriously?" she whispered, incredulous. "*Open Sesame?* I didn't think that would actually *work*!"

"Just like Ali Baba's cave," said Delilah, grinning.

They crept into the kitchen, hearing the soft meows of sleepy cats all over the house. Moving as quickly as they dared, they hurried through the dank hall and up the stairs. Grace felt her heart would beat right out of her chest any minute. Above them, the square hole in the ceiling was blacker than ink.

"Okay," mouthed Grace. "Hold on tight."

Delilah stood on Grace's feet and wrapped her

arms tightly around her shoulders, and Grace murmured something under her breath. There was a tiny jerk at first, and then they began to rise slowly toward the open hatch. Grace furrowed her brow in concentration, keeping her core muscles as tight as possible. It was far too risky to use the rickety old ladder—the squeaking and creaking would wake even the heaviest sleeper—so flying was their only option. Delilah weighed almost nothing, and Grace was able to maintain a steady pace until they landed softly inside the attic.

The box of junk she and the girls had collected as punishment was still sitting near the opening where they'd left it. She rifled carefully through the box while Delilah stuck her head down the hatch, listening for any movement in the house.

"Ah! This is it," Grace whispered, pulling out a Y-shaped object and turning it in her hands. *Balau Dowser*, she thought. *Such a pretty name for such a boring-looking thing.*

She unzipped the front pocket of her hoodie and

tucked the dowser inside. As she got up and turned to leave, she saw a pair of glowing eyes staring at her from the far wall, which made her nearly jump out of her skin. There was an accusatory "meow" and the cat leaped from its perch.

"Let's go," Grace hissed, tugging on Delilah's arm.

The girl balanced herself on Grace's sneakers once more, and they lifted over the wooden border of the hatch and down to the carpet below, landing with a bump. They froze. There was a small sound—the sound of bedclothes stirring, which was coming from a room to their right. This was followed by a low groan and the soft smacking of lips. Then silence.

Grace felt a fire in her chest as they slid down the stairs, desperately trying to hop over lazing cats without falling over one. They made it to the kitchen, and were almost through the back door, when Grace spotted something on the table next to a small leather satchel. It sparkled pink and white, and the bouncy star on top had tiny streamers. It was the glitter pen Grace had won in one of Ms.

Lemon's woodland treasure hunts. She must have been using it and left it behind in her last lesson with Mrs. Quinlan.

Well, she thought, *it is mine.*

She pocketed the pen, but then noticed the end of a tube of lip gloss poking out of the satchel on the table. She pulled out the tube and immediately recognized Rachel's favorite brand and color. Carefully spilling out the rest of the satchel's contents, she saw one of Una's turtle earrings, a hair tie like the ones Adie wore, and a badge with the evil eye symbol, torn from Jenny's schoolbag. Personal possessions of the coven. In the front pocket of the bag she found a coil of rusty wire, a small glass bottle of brown liquid, and a folded sheet of paper. She opened the paper and read,

> *Five girls of brash and willful mind,*
> *Require bridle, rule, and bind,*
> *Their wicked tongues shall ever be,*
> *'Neath Sophrosynic lock and key.*

Delilah caught hold of the piece of paper as it fell out of Grace's hand.

"A binding spell," said Grace. "She's trying to bind our powers. *Why?*"

The floorboards upstairs creaked as something moved across them.

"We have to go," Delilah whispered urgently. "Now!"

Grace grabbed the small bottle from the table and ran outside after Delilah.

In the muddy garden, Grace pulled out the stopper and emptied the contents of the bottle into a clump of weeds. Then she scraped some watery muck into the bottleneck.

"Wait, just a moment!" she said, and hurried back into the house, being careful not to leave any muddy footprints. She filled the bottle at the kitchen sink.

"Mephistopheles," Mrs. Quinlan's voice growled from upstairs. "Stop that infernal racket and get off my bed! You're tearing holes in the blanket."

"Grace!" hissed Delilah. "Come on!"

"Mephis!" the old woman shouted. "Do that again

and you'll go straight to the kitchen and stay there 'til morning. Do you hear me?"

Grace replaced the bottle stopper and shook the contents until it resembled the brown liquid she had thrown out.

"All right, that's it!" roared Mrs. Quinlan. "You asked for it!"

The snarling screech of a cat was followed by the thump of heavy footsteps on the stairs.

"Hurry!" Delilah squealed.

Grace jammed all the items back into the leather satchel, including the glitter pen from her pocket, and raced out the back door behind Delilah. She'd just managed to pull the door shut when Mrs. Quinlan's furious frame thundered into the kitchen.

"Damn cat!" she yelled. There was a snarling *thrump*, then the clicking of tiny claws across the linoleum and scraping as the cat began to scratch at the back door.

"You know where the litter box is!" the woman howled. "Use it!"

The cat continued scratching.

"You're really starting to get on my nerves, Mephis. *What?*"

Her footsteps smacked across the kitchen floor toward the back door.

"Get back!" Grace hissed, dropping to her haunches and flattening herself against the wall. Delilah crouched down beside her, holding her breath.

The door was wrenched open, and Mrs. Quinlan's face shot out to scan the garden. The cat hung by the scruff of the neck from her weathered hand, twisting from side to side as the old woman squinted her eyes and sniffed at the air. Grace didn't even dare to blink as the cat's face turned in her direction and it let out a gurgling growl. Its green eyes stared straight at the two girls.

Mrs. Quinlan snorted impatiently.

"Stupid cat," she said, stepping back inside as the poor animal continued to wriggle and yowl in protest.

As soon as the door was shut, Grace and Delilah took off, racing through Wilton Place and out onto the main road.

✳✳✳

The next day was unexpectedly sunny. Grace sat at the edge of the football field, picking at her lunch, and periodically lifting her face to the warmth with her eyes closed. It was strange how sunshine could make the world feel like a better place, if only for a little while.

"Hey, Grace," a voice said and, a second later, Una plopped down beside her.

"Hey."

"Long time, no see," said Adie, kneeling down on her other side. "Where's Delilah?"

Grace shot her a look.

"I was only wondering," Adie said quickly. "You weren't in the lunchroom, so we figured you must be out here with her."

"But you're on your own," Una said too solemnly. "Do you feel like you *have* to be on your own, Grace?"

"You can calm down with the therapy voice, Una," Grace tutted, rolling her eyes. "I'm not having emotional problems. Delilah gets extra math lessons some lunchtimes, that's all. And it's sunny out, so…"

"We've missed you," Adie said. "Where've you been?"

"Yeah," said Una. "You're missing out on lessons with Ms. Gold. The spells we're learning are sooo amazing. She is *so* cool."

Adie leaned back and swatted Una with her jacket.

"Sorry," said Una. "I didn't mean to… I just mean you should come to the lessons. You'd really like them."

Grace distractedly flattened her sandwiches and rolled them back up in tinfoil.

"How's Jenny doing in the lessons?" she asked.

"Awesome," Una said, waving her hands enthusiastically. "We did this Cloaking spell. And she totally got it, right away. And another time—ow!"

Again Adie's jacket hit its target.

"Ow!" Una said again. "You got me with the zipper! If that had hit my eye, I could have lost *my eye*."

"Jenny's fine," Adie said, ignoring her. "She's calmed down a bit now. She just wants to learn, like the rest of us."

"And set her spells loose on me?" Grace said.

"That was really stupid of her, but it wasn't deliberate. Really, it wasn't."

"And what about freezing Tracy Murphy—wasn't *that* deliberate?"

"So *what* if she froze the Beast?" Una protested. "She deserved it. Besides, it was only temporary, and it's not like she hurt her."

"We want you to come back," Adie interrupted. "Ms. Gold's really worried about the Mirrorman. She says he's incredibly dangerous. She says he has to be destroyed before he comes after us, and he *will* come after us. You know that better than anyone, because it was *you* he tried to get at through the enchanted mirror, right? She needs our help, Grace. *All* of us."

Grace's mind filled with the horrible image she had seen in Mr. Pamuk's shop. The image the Mirrorman had shown her. Her friends, bound and screaming and terrified. She hadn't seen herself in the vision—was that the future if she left them to face him without her? Was she meant to save them? She shifted her weight and felt the Balau Dowser move against her back. She kept it tucked uncomfortably into the waistband of her skirt, afraid to be without it whenever the time spell bounced her back to Beth and Vera and Meredith. She wished she could control the spell and bounce back immediately, give them the dowser, and get the Mirrorman pulled back to his own time. Then all this worry would be over.

"We're going to meet Ms. Gold after last class for training. Please come with us? Just to see what the plan is," said Adie. "*Please?*"

"All right," said Grace. "Just to see what the plan is."

18
in training

The P block was quiet, as usual. Jenny leaned casually against the wall on Grace's right, eyeing her and making no effort to welcome her back.

"Hey, Grace," Rachel said with a little wave. "It's great you could come."

She looked to Jenny as if to elicit a similar greeting, but Jenny said nothing and continued to stare.

"Jenny," a smooth voice said from the shadows at the end of the hall. "A witch, much missed, has returned to your coven. How do you welcome her home?"

Ms. Gold's luminous features were barely visible in the dim light. Jenny inhaled loudly, then pushed herself off the wall and stood in front of Grace, a little too close.

"Welcome back," she said, her voice low and level.

Grace nodded curtly, but couldn't help feeling intimidated. There was something of the Baskerville hound in Jenny's eyes, and it sent pins and needles up Grace's neck.

"Now everything's as it should be," said Ms. Gold, stepping from the shadows. "Let's begin."

She led them into the lab at the very end of the hall, the room farthest from the rest of the school. Inside, black blinds covered the windows, blocking out the fading daylight, and the smell of incense wafted through the air. The lights were left off, but the room was illuminated with several branched candlesticks. Grace thought it all looked a bit ridiculous, but the others seemed to relax in the flickering gloom. Perhaps they had become used to Ms. Gold's dramatic flair during the lessons Grace had missed. They remained solemn and quiet, taking their seats around one table, with Ms. Gold at the head. When

Grace had settled herself next to Adie, Ms. Gold laid her hands on the table, palms up.

"My Wiccan sisters," she said. "May your powers be fierce and your castings triumphant."

"Blessed be," the others said in chorus.

Adie looked at Grace with a little shrug and a grin as if to say, *That's just something we do now.*

Ms. Gold picked up a burning stick of incense and drew a figure eight in the air, over and over, until the snaking line of smoke swelled into a thick band. She replaced the stick in its holder, but the wavy line of smoke continued to move, maintaining its shape in the air. Suddenly the smoke billowed and the Mirrorman's face burst from the center, making them all jump.

"This is the reason we're here," said Ms. Gold. "This creature has the ability and, more importantly, the desire to destroy us all. But I don't want you to be afraid. Don't underestimate how much you have learned and how far you have come. He is more powerful than any *one* of us. But if we work together, if we pool our resources, we are more powerful than him, and can banish him forever."

The Mirrorman's face was swallowed in the cloud of gray, and a smoky matchstick man took its place. The cloud spewed out another six puffs, which formed matchstick figures surrounding the man. He moved sharply, striking out at them but missing as they ducked his attacks.

"We keep him surrounded—that's the key," Ms. Gold continued. "We stay nimble and quick, until he is trapped and contained."

The six misty figures each cast out a strip of laddered smoke. The strips met in the middle, forming a net above the matchstick man's head. The net smacked down in a *whoosh* that dispersed the smoke throughout the room. The girls coughed and waved their hands to clear it. As Grace shook her arm in the air, she noticed Jenny sitting stoically, her eyes watering from the effort, making no attempt to clear the air, but letting the smoke drift over her.

"Then we're ready?" said Jenny. "Ready to crush him before he gets to us?"

"Not yet," said Ms. Gold. "We've been expanding your knowledge, but now we need to hone your reflexes. Now the *real* training begins. Follow me."

Ms. Gold led them out of the school and down the road, following the rough track beside the river as it swerved out and around the woods. Grace felt nervous; if they weren't heading toward the woods, where on earth were they going—and why?

They walked for nearly an hour and, as night fell, the teacher finally guided them off the track, sliding down the grassy bank to the water's edge.

"This is your training ground," she said, spreading her arms in a wide arc.

She lifted a small velvet pouch that hung from her waist and pulled out five white ribbons. Looping the first one around Jenny's neck, she licked her finger and thumb and pressed the two ends together. A small golden seal appeared beneath her thumb, like the wax seals Grace had seen on medieval scrolls in the movies. Inscribed on the seal in beautiful calligraphy was the letter *J*. Ms. Gold arranged it lovingly beside the other charm she'd given Jenny. The teacher then gave each of the girls a ribbon in turn, finally wrapping one around Grace's neck and finishing it with a golden seal inscribed with the letter *G*.

"The aim of the game," she said, "is to collect as many ribbons as possible. You'll battle against each other, using the spells you have in your arsenal, in order to obtain your opponents' ribbons. If your ribbon is taken, you're 'dead,' and must return to this spot until the game is over."

"We're going to fight each other?" asked Adie.

"And me," said Ms. Gold. "Don't look so alarmed. I won't be attacking you directly—but throwing obstacles in your way as you combat each other. Your reflexes must become superfast, and your casting instantaneous. And you must learn to do this with any number of distractions."

"What are the rules of the game?" Grace asked as a knot began to twist in her stomach.

"There are no rules," the teacher replied, smiling. "You use the powers you have and collect as many ribbons as you can. Everyone ready?"

"Scary, isn't it?" Adie whispered to Grace. "But fun!"

"Everyone ready?" Ms. Gold repeated, trotting a few feet away. "Then let the game begin!"

The girls stood uncertainly until Ms. Gold flicked her hands and strings of weeds shot out from the bank gripping the girls' ankles. They shrieked and jumped into action—Adie and Una took off downstream, while the other three leaped into the air.

Grace somersaulted backward, twisting off the writhing plant that had hold of her leg, and shot across the water, stopping to hover over the river. Rachel had soared into the sky and could no longer be seen, while Jenny rested some way up from Grace, looking down with a sneer that made Grace's stomach lurch. The clouds above them suddenly darkened, and one glance at the figure on the shore made it clear Ms. Gold's distractions had begun. Jenny took one more look at Grace, before shooting upward in search of Rachel.

Grace knew she was at a disadvantage. With only a few spells she could confidently use, the others had her outgunned. She felt ashamed to think of it, but she knew Una would be her easiest target.

There was a sudden crack of thunder and a bolt of lightning pierced the water just inches from her feet. She swung herself horizontal to the water and took off after Adie and Una. In the distance, she could make out Adie's curls flattening against her back in dark streaks as the rain pelted down. She increased her speed, squinting her eyes against the stinging rain. Adie was still running and hadn't seen her. She could catch her before her friend even knew she was there.

She reached her hand forward but something hit her shoulder, knocking her out of her flight path and sending her tumbling across the bank.

"Whoops, sorry!" said Una's voice. "You okay?"

Grace rubbed some muck from her cheek and nodded. She looked up, but couldn't see Una anywhere.

"Una! Where are you?"

The only reply was a little giggle and shuffling in the leaves ahead of her.

Grace couldn't help grinning and leaped into hiding behind a drooping willow tree. Quick as a flash, she originated a black otter on a leash. The animal moved swiftly through the vegetation, twitching its nose as Grace silently ordered it to sniff out the competition. Without warning, the otter froze, its sleek body flattening to the ground.

In front of it, Grace could see two muddy footprints. The rain cascaded on either side of them, yet they didn't fill with water. Smiling, she thanked her little companion and dismissed him with a wave. Then, ducking to her haunches at the side of the pathway, she waited for Una to come to her.

After a few moments, the footprints sucked in water, and new prints formed in front of them. When Una was nearly beside her, Grace jumped out, grasping at the air and, wrapping her arms around Una's invisible shoulders, she tackled her to the ground and tickled her until her friend squealed with laughter. Then, feeling for the ribbon at her neck, she pulled and snapped the seal. The ribbon appeared in Grace's hand, and Una's protesting face appeared below her.

"No fair!" Una said.

"Sorry, Una," Grace said, tucking the ribbon into her pocket. "That Cloaking spell was awesome, though!"

The praise didn't improve Una's mood, and she shrugged Grace off and trudged back toward Ms. Gold.

"Sorry, Una!" Grace called again.

She turned to try and pick up Adie's trail and immediately spotted a mini tidal wave thundering across the river toward her. She scaled the bank as the wave crashed to shore, splashing her jeans as she continued to scramble upward.

"You all right?"

As the water retreated, she could see Adie's rain-soaked figure a little farther downstream.

"Jeez, Adie," she complained. "Yeah, I'm okay, but go easy."

"Sorry," Adie shouted back in reply, "but don't worry. I've got good control over water."

As Grace slid down the bank toward her, she could see her friend was telling the truth. Grace readied herself for flight as Adie made circles in the air with her fingertips, coaxing the falling rain into a spinning vortex. The swirling cage of water made a sudden rush toward Grace. Flipping into the air, she managed to get above it, then dove toward Adie with her arms outstretched. She was just within reach when a bolt of lightning cracked between them, so close that Grace could feel its heat. She toppled sideways into the river, which immediately swelled around her, forming a seat that held her tightly. Her watery throne rode like a wave toward Adie waiting on the shore.

Grace resigned herself to being "dead" and relaxed into the river chair that soaked her clothes, before spying something moving along the bank. She opened her mouth to warn Adie, but she was too slow.

Jenny uncloaked and directed the hanging branches

of a tree to slide around Adie's waist, pinning her arms to her side and binding her knees together. Adie looked shocked as Jenny snapped the ribbon from around her neck.

"Where did you learn how to—" was all Grace heard before the swelling water collapsed underneath her and she sank beneath the surface.

She heard Adie's muffled scream from under the water and surfaced to see her friend, now free, running into the river. Jenny was nowhere to be seen.

"I'm so sorry!" Adie shouted, as she waded in up to her knees. "I forgot to hold on to you!"

Grace did an awkward front crawl until she could feel sandy gravel beneath her feet.

"It's all right," she said. "Go on back to Ms. Gold."

"You sure?"

"I'm okay. See you back there when it's over."

She watched Adie make her way upstream, then leaned over and gripped her knees, coughing up the last of the silty water that she had swallowed.

"Grace."

She looked up to see Ms. Gold standing on the bank. She was holding her hand out.

"It's not over, Miss," Grace said, coughing again. "I've still got my ribbon. Look."

"It *is* over, Grace," Ms. Gold said. "This has gotten a little more competitive than I'd like. I'm calling time."

Grace was surprised at her own disappointment. Jenny had at least one ribbon, but so did she. She still had a chance to win.

"Let's go." Ms. Gold flapped her hand to hurry her along.

As Grace jogged toward the teacher, she spotted the little velvet bag hanging from her waist and smiled to herself. She picked up speed but, before Ms. Gold could grab her hand, she vaulted over the woman's head, landing behind her to tuck her hand into her collar and snap the unseen ribbon from her neck.

"Fudge!" the fake Ms. Gold shouted, spinning around. "How did you *know*?"

Grace smiled as Ms. Gold's luminosity melted away to reveal Rachel's unusually flushed cheeks.

"The bag was on a belt loop on her *left*, not her right."

"Fudge!"

"You said that already," Grace said, still smiling. "That was good, though, Rach. *Really* good."

Rachel grunted in reply and marched upstream, where Grace could just make out the real Ms. Gold, standing with Adie and Una on either side. She felt the flutter of butterflies in her tummy as she realized Jenny was the only one left.

"It's just you and me now."

There she was, on the opposite side of the river, that now familiar sneer curling her lip, and her eyes colder than Grace had ever seen. Before either of them could move, there was a screeching sound as something sailed toward them in the rain, stopping to spin in the air above them. Another of Ms. Gold's distractions. It looked like the wheel of a wooden cart but, as it spun, Grace could see sharp-edged, star-shaped objects spitting from its spokes. One of them shot toward her, glancing off her shoulder.

"Ow!" she yelled, as a ripple of pain spread across her back and down her body.

Across the river, she could see Jenny buckling over with the same pain. But Grace was the first to recover. She straightened and turned just in time to see a creeping weed rush out of the undergrowth and snatch her ankle. Two more stars glanced off her knee and right arm, but as Grace began to fall, one of the stars ricocheted, slicing through the plant that held her leg. She scrambled to her feet.

From across the river, it looked like Jenny had gained control of every tree, plant, and weed. There was a massive rustling of foliage before what looked like the entire bank reared up and lunged for Grace. She launched herself into the sky, reeling against the impact of more shooting stars, before diving headfirst into the river.

The pressure of the water felt like a protective cush-ion. Grace jerked horizontal to skim speedily along the river bottom, planning to stay under for as long as her breath would allow. Within seconds, though, the pressure had changed; she felt the river pushing at her from behind. Something massive was forming in the water. She turned around to face a giant set of jaws, lined with jagged teeth.

The creature behind her had a huge serpentlike body that moved through the water at terrific speed. Grace looked up. In a flash she had opened the sphere of a brand-new companion above the surface of the river. Through the glassy murkiness, she could see its pointed head and enormous scaly body readying itself, before it sliced down through the water, plunging its teeth into the neck of Jenny's serpent.

Grace's lungs were now screaming for oxygen, but she was swept, powerless, in the surging water as the dragon and serpent battled each other. Churning in the raging rapids, her head felt heavy, spots were appearing before her eyes, and she knew she was losing consciousness. With her last clear thought, she begged for help.

The very next moment, she was rocketing out of the water, the wonderful relief of cool air filling her lungs, and her dragon at her back. Remaining airborne for a moment, she turned to see her scaly companion dropping beneath her, his eyes fixed on hers. Suddenly, he shrieked in pain as Jenny's serpent clenched its jaws around his scaly tail, almost tearing it from his body. Shakily raising her hand, Grace waved over the shrieking dragon, and he popped into nothing, revealing the gaping mouth of the serpent beneath. Now almost numb with weakness, Grace pushed herself back into the air, narrowly avoiding the snapping jaws and, with one last effort, threw herself onto the far shore. She hit the ground hard and rolled to a stop. With the wind knocked out of her, she could do nothing for a moment but gasp for breath and feel the soreness that pulsed from her head to her feet.

When she could breathe again, Grace turned onto her back and grimaced. She reached behind her and pulled out the Balau Dowser that had managed to stay lodged in her waistband during the whole ordeal. She held it up to her face, but her eyes focused past it on a figure in the sky, silhouetted against the moon. It was Jenny—and she was plunging headfirst toward her.

With lightning speed, Grace wrenched the hair tie from her hair and snatched a pebble from the ground. Jenny was just yards away when Grace snapped the hair tie over the dowser, and fired the pebble from the makeshift slingshot. The stone struck Jenny's cheek, and she fell to the bank, screaming and clutching her face. Before she could recover, Grace scrambled over, on her hands and knees, and snapped the ribbon from her neck.

Collapsing onto her heels, she heaved a sigh of relief. It was over.

Ms. Gold and the others joined them on the far bank.

"She cheated," Jenny hissed, as Grace tucked the dowser out of sight.

"There were no rules to break, remember?" she said.

Ms. Gold took a long look at Jenny, still curled on the ground, nursing the deep cut on her cheek.

"Tomorrow," the teacher said. "We will eliminate him tomorrow."

19
a rude awakening

"Grace! Wake up!"

Grace's eyes were sticky with sleep as they blinked open.

"Grace!" her mom called again.

Her bedroom curtains were closed, but there was plenty of light. Grace guessed it was late morning or early afternoon.

"Yeah, Mom?" she croaked.

"Your friend's here to see you…" She heard her mom's voice quiet before she shouted again. "It's Delilah."

Grace frowned. Delilah had never come to her house before. For a split second she saw the Delilah from her nightmare—at Vera's side, stabbing her with a dagger. She shivered and tipped her feet onto the floor.

"Hurry up, honey," her mom called. "I'm not spending all day shouting at you from down here."

Grace pulled on a pair of jeans and a hoodie and quickly brushed her teeth in the bathroom. Almost as an afterthought, she shoved the dowser into the waistband of her jeans. Downstairs, Delilah was standing just inside the front door.

"Your friend insisted on waiting for you at the door." Grace's mom smiled. "And won't let me tempt her with some cookies or orange juice. Are you sure there's nothing you'd like, sweetheart?"

Delilah shook her head shyly and Grace's mom shrugged.

"Oh, well, I tried," she said. "I'm heading out to the backyard now to put those azaleas in. Lovely to meet you, Delilah."

When they were alone, Delilah grabbed Grace's sleeve and looked up at her earnestly.

"I have to show you something," she whispered.

Grace could feel Delilah's hand shaking on her hoodie, and her eyes were even wider than usual. She was nervous.

"What is it?"

The small girl shook her head.

"I can't tell you. I have to show you."

Twenty minutes later, and Grace could barely keep up with her young friend as they raced across the rickety wooden bridge and down the road that led to Delilah's house. They turned in to the muddy path between trees that blocked out most of the daylight. Even in the early afternoon sunshine, the run-down house looked just as dark as it had the first time Grace had seen it.

"I can't stay long," Grace said breathlessly. "Ms. Gold says we're going after the Mirrorman tonight, and I still haven't gotten the dowser to Beth and Meredith. It's going to be a close one."

The other girl didn't reply, but lit the oil lamp on the porch and hurried inside. At the back of the house the familiar moldy smell permeated the kitchen, but the table had been pushed to one side and a single chair remained in the center of the room.

"Sit down," the girl said, "and I'll be right back."

Puzzled, Grace took the offered seat and waited. A few minutes passed.

"Delilah," she called impatiently. "I told you I can't wait around. Ms. Gold—"

"Ms. Gold, what?"

Grace jumped. In the darkness of the far corner she saw something move and a figure emerge from the shadows.

"Ms. Gold!" said Grace, perplexed.

"It's good to see you again so soon, Grace," the teacher said. "I was very impressed with your performance yesterday. Impressed and, I have to say, rather surprised."

"But what are you—"

Suddenly, an odd sensation shot through Grace's mouth, and her tongue stopped moving. The same feeling crept from her toes and her fingertips—a stinging numbness like she'd just come in out of the freezing cold and her hands and feet were warming up too quickly.

"You're a fast thinker," the woman went on, ignoring Grace's distress, "and your reflexes aren't bad. It's a shame, really."

The numbness had spread throughout Grace's body, as far as her neck. She willed her arms to move, but they were useless. Her head tipped to one side, and she could see Delilah standing frozen, just outside the kitchen door, with a silk scarf in her hands. Grace tried to signal for her to run, but the rest of her face had succumbed to the stinging paralysis.

"I'm afraid you'll be staying here for a while." Ms. Gold sauntered in front of her chair, examining her fingernails. "The lash, Delilah."

Ms. Gold looked up, as if talking to the wall behind Grace.

"The *lash*, child!"

"Yes, Mother," the tiny voice replied.

Mother? A gurgled cry of disbelief escaped Grace's throat. Delilah approached her with the scarf and, avoiding her gaze, wrapped it around her shoulders and secured it at her back. The silk felt solid, like a steel chain cutting into Grace's arms.

"There," Ms. Gold said. "We can be a little more civilized now."

The numbness lifted, and Grace could feel her limbs again, but she remained firmly tied to the chair. Struggling to speak, she found she could barely mumble.

"Why? Why are you doing this?"

The woman smiled.

"I would have liked for you to join your friends in our little adventure this evening," she said, her wide grin revealing her perfect, white teeth, "but I have a terrible feeling you've been keeping something from me. You see, Creepy Bob was a thorn in my side many years ago. But I removed that thorn. So tell me this, little one..."

She leaned over and gazed into Grace's eyes, that horrible grin still lighting up her face.

"Who set him free?"

Grace glanced at Delilah, but the girl stared fixedly at the floor. Ms. Gold gently swept a stray strand of hair behind Grace's ear.

"She can't help you, little one. Just tell me the truth, and I'll let you go. I promise."

The woman stood up and drew a glowing *X* over her heart with one finger.

"Cross. My. Heart."

"I don't know." Grace's voice cracked.

"Was it Beth?"

Grace shook her head.

"Vera?"

Another shake of the head.

"*You?*"

"I don't know who set him free."

The luminous cheeks flushed red for a split second.

"Then you are going to be here for a very, very long time."

Hours later, Ms. Gold was gone, and the shadows had moved across the kitchen floor with the sun. It was twilight now, and there was very little light in the room.

Grace ached all over, still strapped into the chair, and was getting light-headed with hunger and worry. Once more, she focused on the rotting wooden table and tried to originate a new companion that could snap her silk binding. But, once again, the sphere fizzled to nothing before she could set the animal free.

"It won't work," a small voice said. "The lash won't let you."

Delilah's brown eyes peeked from around the doorframe.

"I thought you left with your...*mother*," Grace said bitterly. The small girl shook her head.

"I'm supposed to keep an eye on you."

Grace wriggled against the lash.

"The least you could do is loosen it—just a little? It *hurts*."

She gave an exaggerated look of pain, but dropped

it when the girl didn't budge from her spot outside the door. She tried another tack.

"Delilah, you lied to her. You didn't tell her where the Mirrorman came from," said Grace. "Why?"

"She's afraid of him."

"And you want her to be afraid?"

Delilah shrugged.

"If you let me go, we can stop her from destroying him," said Grace. "Then she'll stay afraid."

"I can't let you go."

"Please!" Grace begged.

"I can't break the lash."

Grace's shoulders sagged against the silk scarf, and the pressure made her head even lighter. A single tear dropped from her face and landed on her knee.

"I really thought you were my friend."

Delilah stood watching her from the doorjamb, then turned away and disappeared into the house.

Grace drifted reluctantly into sleep and dreamed. But not peacefully.

She was back in the scene the Mirrorman had

shown her—Adie and Rachel on their knees with their hands bound, a momentary image of Una with her head bowed, screaming and crying. But Grace wasn't just watching this time. She could *feel* everything, like she was really there. She could feel how terrified they were; she could hear their screams as if they were coming from inside her own head. But she was useless. She was so close to them, but she couldn't reach them. Her arms wouldn't move and her legs were frozen. Then Adie lifted her head and the look of horror on her face made Grace's blood run cold. All at once, Grace was in front of the enchanted mirror, watching the face with one blue eye and one staring white. His mouth stretched in a discordant scream, and his face launched at her.

"Nooo!" Grace screamed into the darkness.

She awoke. She was still in the kitchen, and it was night. Her neck was stiff, and the muscles screamed when she lifted her head. As she stretched against the soreness, she heard the far-off sound of a train.

Grace's head snapped to attention, despite the

wrenching pain, and she listened intently. The train kept coming.

Clickety-click-click.

Clickety-click-click.

She closed her eyes and crossed her fingers.

Clickety-click-click.

Clickety-click-click.

Her prayers were answered. The foghorn blast reverberated through the kitchen, the chair disappeared beneath her, and she landed in muck on the woodland floor.

✳✳✳

Adie leaned against the wall of the P block, tugging nervously at the beaded bracelets around her wrists.

"How do these keep us safe, Miss?" she asked.

"They're a simple repellent, Adie," Ms. Gold replied. "He won't like to go near them, so please make sure you keep them on your wrists at all times."

Adie glanced at Rachel, who shrugged, tugging

at her own bracelets. Una sat cross-legged on the floor, watching intently as Ms. Gold finished drawing an oblong diamond shape around the mouth of the demon well. One point was much higher than the others and decorated with ornate swirls. When the symbol was complete, Jenny placed white stones at each of the plainer points.

"Why is that one part all fancy, Miss?" asked Una.

"It's where I'll stand, Una," replied Ms. Gold, "as leader of the coven."

"And he'll just come to us?" said Adie.

"Yes."

"How come there are only three other points?"

"Jenny will stand behind me."

"How will she cast her part of the net over him if she's behind you?" Adie heard the teacher take a deep breath and exhale.

"Miss?" she asked again. "How—"

"*Enough!*" Ms. Gold's voice echoed through the empty block.

Adie felt the prickle of goose bumps down her arms.

"Enough questions," the teacher said finally. "Everyone take your places."

Una glanced nervously at Adie and Rachel before hurrying to take her spot on the diamond.

"Where's Grace?" Rachel whispered to Adie as they made their way toward the mouth of the well.

"I don't know," Adie whispered back. "I don't like this."

"It'll be okay." Rachel placed a comforting hand on her arm. "Ms. Gold knows what she's doing."

Adie watched the teacher as she took her spot on the diamond. Ms. Gold's breathing was measured and, more than once, Adie saw the shadow of a smirk cross her face. It seemed like excitement. Adie didn't feel excited, she just felt nervous. She couldn't understand why Grace hadn't shown up and why Ms. Gold seemed perfectly happy to go ahead without her. After all, Grace had won the game by the river. Didn't they need her?

"You three," said the teacher. "On your knees."

Adie frowned. She tried to make eye contact

with Jenny, but Jenny was behind Ms. Gold with her head down.

"On your knees"—there was a tremor in Ms. Gold's voice now—"until the verses are read. This is important."

Adie watched Rachel and Una slowly lower to the ground, and then followed them. She felt insecure and unprepared, kneeling. She wanted to be on her feet, ready to spring into the air the second the Mirrorman appeared. She wanted Grace beside her—Grace, with her quick reflexes and good sense. Unable to meet the gaze of any of her friends, Adie suddenly felt very alone.

✳✳✳

Back in 1977, Grace was sprinting through the woods toward the hut. She had already adopted her Grayanna disguise. She scoped out the surroundings of the hut and tiptoed to the door to listen for voices. All she could hear were Beth's soothing words to Vera. Meredith was nowhere to be seen.

Beth jumped at the sound of Grace entering the hut, but then smiled sadly when she saw who it was. Grace tried to hide her shock at the sight of Vera. The girl was completely motionless now, and her skin was turning gray. She looked cold. She looked *dead*.

"I try to keep her as warm as I can," Beth said, pulling a blanket tighter to Vera's shoulders, and giving Grace a helpless look, "but she stays cold. It won't be much longer, and then no one will be able to help her. Did you bring the dowser?"

Grace pulled it from her waistband and Beth grabbed it.

"We can bring him back now! We can bring him back and he'll break Vera's binding."

She pulled the Mirrorman's fishing fly from her pocket and lodged the hook into one arm of the dowser.

Grace's heart was sinking. She didn't want her friends to go up against the Mirrorman with Ms. Gold—for all she knew, the teacher was planning to sacrifice them to the fight—but she didn't want anything to happen to Beth either. Vera, she had to admit, looked as if she was lost already.

"Where's Meredith?" she asked.

"Took off again," Beth replied. "She pops in every once in a while, but never for long. She keeps saying she has stuff to do."

"What stuff?"

"Who knows? It's Meredith. She never tells you everything. But we need to find her for the casting."

"No!" Grace started, before calming herself. "We have to go ahead without her. I...I can't explain it, but we need to do it now. You said yourself, Vera's running out of time."

Beth watched her closely.

"All right," she said at last.

They stood in the dark outside the hut. The wind had picked up and the night was getting colder—there was a storm on the way. Beth had wedged the dowser, with the fishing fly still stuck in one arm, into the soil. She sprinkled the concoction she and Vera had made days earlier around the dowser, spiraling outward until the container was empty.

"All right," she said, looking much more herself now that she was filled with hope. "You stand here and be ready to help him when he comes through the portal. The journey will probably leave him a bit shaken for a few minutes."

A bit shaken, Grace thought, *maybe long enough for me and Beth to forget this and make a run for it.*

But that would leave Vera alone, and doomed, in the hut. Grace chewed on her lip with guilt and fear.

The first few drops of rain were beginning to fall, and the wind blew in all directions, whipping leaves and branches into a frenzy.

"Ready?" Beth shouted over the weather.

"What?" Grace could barely hear her, though she was no more than ten yards away.

"You ready?"

"Yep," Grace said inaudibly, but gave Beth an exaggerated nod.

Beth smiled and raised her arms above her head,

calling out a verse that Grace couldn't hear. The rain began to pour in earnest, and the wind snapped Grace's hair from side to side. She watched the space above the dowser and jumped as it made a sudden and loud *craaaack*! She could see a split in the air, like a crack in the world, which pushed and widened. The space around it swelled and stretched, fighting against the unnatural break, but the crevice grew. The sound was earsplitting, even over the howling wind.

"Beth!" Grace started to panic. "You have to be careful. Be careful when he comes through!"

But Beth couldn't hear her over the din. Grace could make out her hopeful gaze as she watched the portal break open. Then two things happened at once.

A figure, wrapped in glossy black, tumbled through the portal and landed in front of the dowser. At the same moment, Grace saw a flash of golden blond, and suddenly Meredith was gripping the dowser, wrenching the fishing fly from the wood. The black figure growled and reached for the fly, but Meredith was too quick.

"Meredith, wait!" Beth cried, running at her. "What are you doing? We need his help!"

Meredith raised her hands, and Beth was suddenly rolling backward into the trees. The blond girl swung around to Grace, but Grace had seen this trick from Ms. Gold before. She dove into the undergrowth and felt the invisible blow shake the leaves around her. Meredith started running, but Grace launched herself forward and gripped her ankles, tackling her to the ground.

"Let go!" the girl snarled, her eyes burning with rage.

Grace felt the tickle of something traveling up her leg and back, circling her neck. Meredith's eyes narrowed and the vine tightened around Grace's throat.

"*Let go!*"

Grace refused to loosen her grip, and the vine wound itself even tighter. Her head swam, but then a sudden weight fell on her back, and fingers started grabbing at the plant around her throat. She gasped in pain as the fingers roughly pulled at her neck, snapping the vine. She took great gulps of air.

Meredith feverishly kicked off Grace's grip, scrambling away from the figure in the black hood before he could fully regain his balance.

Grace was lifted to her feet, still gasping.

"Slow breaths," a gravelly, whispery voice said. "Slower, or you'll pass out."

She took two or three more breaths before turning to look at the Mirrorman in the face. He was so close, she could make out the pores in his ashen cheeks, each wispy hair on his head.

"The blond witch," he growled. "She has my jewel."

Grace numbly shook her head.

"The fly," he said loudly. "My fishing fly."

"We needed something of yours," Grace stammered, "to bring you back."

"Where will she go?"

Grace shook her head again.

"I don't know."

Just then there was a pained groan far behind them.

"Beth!" Grace cried, racing over to where the girl had landed after Meredith's attack.

Beth lay curled up on the ground, holding one hand to her forehead where there was a trickle of blood.

"God, Beth," Grace said. "Are you okay?"

"Meredith," Beth mumbled. "Why did she…?"

Her words drifted into nothing and she groaned again.

"She needs rest." The Mirrorman's voice was dry and flat behind them. "She needs to be out of the rain."

Grace was about to reply that she couldn't carry Beth all the way out of the woods, when the old man pushed past her, lifted Beth in his arms, and brought her back to the hut.

Ducking through the doorway, he paused for a second, before plunking Beth down beside Vera. He stood and stared at the figurine in the spiky-haired girl's hand with a dark look on his face.

"Please release her," Beth croaked, reaching her hand to her head again. "We didn't mean any harm coming here—she doesn't deserve this."

The Mirrorman furrowed his brow.

"This is not my binding," he said.

"Not yours?" Grace said from the doorway. "But it was in the soil just outside. It was meant for anyone who came near the hut. It was meant…"

Grace watched his face as he continued to stare at the doll in Vera's hand.

"It was meant for *you*," she whispered.

"The blond witch," he said sternly to Beth. "Where will she go?"

Tears filled Beth's eyes, and a sorrowful sound escaped her throat.

"Meredith?" she said. "Meredith did this?"

"Where?" he repeated.

"There's no time left!" Beth sobbed, gripping Vera's hand. "Only the caster can break the spell."

Or a Wiccan virtuoso, Grace thought.

The Mirrorman pounced on Beth suddenly, holding her by the front of her sweater.

"Tell me where she is," he hissed, "and *I* will break the binding!"

Beth's tears spilled down her cheeks and splashed onto her hands, but her face hardened.

"Break the binding *now*," she said firmly, "and I'll tell you what you need to know."

Still holding on to her, the Mirrorman's free hand snatched the figurine, with Vera's fingers clamped around it. His knuckles went white with the pressure, and two streams of bright red blood ran down either side of his wrist. Grace couldn't tell if the blood was his or Vera's, but the brass sticks of the ornament were cutting into someone's skin. Beth held his gaze, unblinking, as he mumbled with furious speed through gritted teeth. It was several minutes before the murmuring stopped, and he peeled his fingers from the brass doll. Beth kept her lips clamped together until she saw Vera unclench her own hand and let the figurine roll away from her fingers.

"Vera!" She eased her friend's head and shoulders onto her lap and stroked her hair. Color flooded Vera's cheeks and eyes, and her head rolled from side to side as she blinked and groaned awake. Beth looked up at the Mirrorman.

"Thank you," she whispered.

"Where—"

"The demon well," Beth replied instantly, "by the school. She's obsessed with the power of it. She'll go there."

He was gone before she'd finished speaking, and the realization hit Grace like a truck. Ms. Gold said she had gotten rid of Creepy Bob years back—Meredith had planted the Muerte figurine to lure him after her. She had been preparing for his destruction all along. He was running into a trap.

Grace took off after him but, though he looked like a withered old man, the Mirrorman moved through the woods like a cat. She soon lost sight of him in the distance, but she kept running. The wind was blowing against her, and by the time she reached the edge of the woods, near the school, her legs were like jelly.

And then, she caught sight of them, facing each other across the patch of ground that was the demon well.

"The jewel," she heard him growl over the storm.

Meredith stood with the shimmering fly held out in one hand.

"Here it is," she said. "Take it!"

"Wait!" Grace screamed, breaking into a run again. "It's a trap!"

The Mirrorman turned at the sound of her voice and, from nowhere, Meredith hurled a net of smoke that enveloped him and pulled him to the ground. In an instant, she had dragged him over to where the mouth of the well was. She crushed a glass container under her foot, and liquid flooded from the breakage and seeped into the ground, which began to bubble and sink beneath the weight of the Mirrorman. He fought against the net, but it snaked around his limbs as he struggled. Beams of red light spiked from the grass around him. The demon well was opening.

"No!" Grace cried, throwing herself to the ground and gripping one end of the smoky net. She tried to drag him away from the well, but a sudden punch to the face sent her sprawling. A second later, Meredith had her pinned to the ground, holding down her wrists and grinning. The jeweled fly was hooked onto her shirt, its orange eye glinting in the moonlight.

"It's over, *Grayanna*," she hissed. "No one can stop me now."

Grace's cries mingled with the Mirrorman's as the red light engulfed him, and he was swallowed by the demon well. The red mouth of the well snapped shut.

Under his fading cries and the gleeful, triumphant roar of Meredith, Grace could hear the sound of a train. As light swelled around her, she slipped one hand from Meredith's grip and snatched the fly from her shirt. She saw the girl's look of horror, before the foghorn blast sent her racing into the future.

20

from the well

Adie kept her hands on the ground as she kneeled on the floor; she was certain she could feel the ground getting warmer. Ms. Gold had shrieked words in another language, but now she was silent. And smiling.

"You girls," she said at last, "have the honor of being part of something extraordinary. A new age, a new beginning, a new *world*."

The woman looked nothing like her usual composed self. Her hair was unkempt, and she looked barely able to stand with the nervous tremors that gripped her whole body.

"I had the chance once," she breathed, "to become the

most powerful being on Earth. And it was snatched from me. But now..."

Adie's heart fluttered with panic as the woman gasped for breath.

"But *now*," Ms. Gold continued, "I will have an army more powerful than any witch's trinket. My own army. My *demon* army!"

Before Adie could move, the beaded bracelets on her wrists pulled together, like the strongest of magnets, snapping her arms behind her back. She tried to roll away from her place on the diamond, but she couldn't. It was as if her knees were glued to the spot.

"Rachel!" she cried.

"I can't move, Adie," Rachel cried in reply. "Oh God, what's happening?"

"Jenny!" Una's face was already dripping with tears, as she struggled against the bracelets gripping her wrists. "Help us!"

But Jenny didn't even look at her three friends. She kept her head down, standing quietly behind Ms. Gold, as the teacher's triumphant chants grew more frenzied.

Adie's gaze fixed on the center of the diamond, where red cracks were appearing in the floor. Her eyes widened in horror.

"The well," she gasped. "It's opening!"

✳✳✳

Grace blinked against the blast of sound that landed her back in her own time. She was by a door in a dark corner of the P block. Through it, she could see she had bounced right into the scene the Mirrorman had shown her—the image of her nightmares.

Jenny was immediately in front, with her back to Grace, right behind Ms. Gold. The other three were on their knees, hands bound behind their backs, screaming. Adie was in the center, her face illuminated by red shafts of light that were streaming from the site of the demon well.

Grace gripped the fishing fly in her hand, not even feeling the hook pierce her palm. She rushed forward, plowing into Jenny and sending her and Ms. Gold sprawling across the floor. She spun around, in time to see Ms. Gold raise her hands, but not in time to avoid the invisible strike that followed. She hit the wall with horrible force and sank to the ground, dazed. The ceiling was spinning above her as Ms. Gold's luminous face came into view.

"Little Miss Resourceful, aren't you?" Ms. Gold raised her hands for another hit, but stopped short when she saw what was in Grace's hand. "The *jewel*!"

Grace readied herself to fly, concentrating hard so she wouldn't go too high or too far. But just as she focused her mind, the fly's feathers fluttered against her skin and she took off at ferocious speed, crashing through the double doors of the P block and rolling to a messy stop in the C block. Stunned, she clambered to her feet, watching the feathers settle in her palm.

"Grace!" Adie screamed helplessly through the heavy doors. Grace ran toward them, but they were suddenly blown from their hinges, and Ms. Gold emerged in a mini-cyclone that fired debris in all directions.

"Finally"—the woman's voice sounded strangely

discordant—"I will have it all! I will be the most powerful witch the world has ever seen, with a demon army at my command! And *you*, little one"—she grinned, reaching for Grace—"will be a loyal soldier."

She rushed forward, grabbing Grace by the throat and flashing her beautiful smile.

"At last!" she hissed.

Her amber eyes were all Grace could see as the world began to fade out.

"Drop her, blondie," a voice said.

A beam of light struck Ms. Gold's head, knocking her and Grace to the ground. As she regained her balance, Grace watched what looked like a glowing boomerang swing around, and then return to the outstretched hand of Mrs. Vera Quinlan. Her heart leaped with joy as the Cat Lady jogged toward them, followed by Ms. Lemon, and, very far behind, Delilah. On spotting the tiny girl, Ms. Gold roared.

"Child! I'll *end you!*"

Delilah stopped, as if frozen, at the end of the hallway.

But Ms. Lemon and Mrs. Quinlan kept on

coming. When they reached Ms. Gold, there was a ferocious eruption of light and sound as all three began throwing magical strikes. Ms. Lemon fended off Ms. Gold's sonic boom blasts, while Mrs. Quinlan flung the glowing boomerang like a ninja, striking her target almost every time. Ms. Gold hit the ground hard, rolling to a stop before stretching her hands out to the side.

"You always feared me, Vera." She spat the words from her mouth. "And you had good reason."

"I couldn't stand you, trollop," Mrs. Quinlan replied. "There's a difference."

Ms. Gold grinned, wriggling her raised fingers, and there was an almighty crash. Distended tree roots and branches smashed through the windows of the hallway and even through parts of the block walls, stretching out to wind themselves around Ms. Gold's enemies. Grace left the two women to fight off the attack, leaping under and over branches, and racing through the open doorway to the P block.

The cracks above the demon well had spread and

joined, so almost the entire circle glowed with red light. Black misty arms thrashed beneath the surface as demons fought to be the first to escape. Grace wrapped her arms around Adie's shoulders and tried to drag her from the spot, but a shard of pain shot through her head. Followed by another and another. With each stab came a vision—the enchanted mirror, a black figure chasing her through the woods, Meredith's triumphant cry by the demon well. She looked down, her heart thumping at the sight of all those demon bodies clashing.

But among them was something else. A face buried in the red light, with one blue eye and one white. He reached his hand toward her.

Before she could react, she was thrown to one side. Jenny lodged one knee in her stomach, holding her down. With a vicious grin, she focused her attention behind Grace, and within seconds Grace could feel the breath of the Baskerville hound on her head.

"No, Jenny!" Una sobbed.

"Stop it, Jenny!" Adie's voice joined her. "Why are you doing this?"

Hot saliva dripped on Grace's cheek and rolled into her hair. The hound could barely wait for its master's command.

"I'm doing this," Jenny sneered, barely loud enough for Grace to hear, "because Ms. Gold will rule the world. And *I'll* be her right hand." She bent close to Grace. "Bye-bye, Grace."

As Jenny leaned over, the bronze charm that Ms. Gold had given her slipped from under her collar, and Grace knew what she had to do. Gripping the fishing fly tight in her hand, she scraped the hook hard along Jenny's leg. With the other hand, she snatched the bronze charm, pulling Jenny on top of her as the hound leaped forward. Unable to hurt its master, it bounced off Jenny's back, and Grace snapped the charm from her neck. The girl fell backward, blinking and gasping for breath.

A deep, guttural growl rolled through the floor, and Grace wondered if the few seconds she had were going to be enough to originate a beast of her own. The hound answered her question by hurtling toward her, dripping jaws wide open. She braced herself for the impact but, with inches to spare, the beast popped into nothing.

"I'm so sorry!" Tears were pouring down Jenny's face as she dragged herself off the floor. "I'm so sorry, Grace! I don't know—"

"No time for that now!" Grace yelled. "We have to get them away from the well!"

Demon arms were now stretching beyond the mouth of the well, gripping the carpet with their misty claws. Moving swiftly, Jenny began snapping off the beaded bracelets that held her friends. But in the midst of demon limbs, Grace could still make out the Mirrorman's outstretched hand.

"I have to get him out," she shouted over the growing howls of the demons below. "Hold on to me and don't let go!"

"You can't!" Jenny said. "They'll grab you!"

Jenny was right. Grace knew she wouldn't be able to pull the Mirrorman out before a demon would grab hold and try to take possession of her body. But she had to try.

She leaned over the mouth of the well and reached in. His hand was grasping for hers. At that moment, she felt the flutter of feathers in her palm again. The closer she leaned toward him, the more frantic the jeweled fly became. She dropped to her stomach and reached farther into the well.

"Grace, no!"

The redness inside the well burned like intense sunlight. Her skin felt instantly tight and dry, but she leaned even farther in. A demon gripped her arm, then another and another. But something—something magical—was preventing them from disappearing into her flesh and taking possession. She could feel the jeweled fly pulsing in her left hand and suddenly understood. She reached in as far as she could with her right.

Frustrated, the demons tried again and again to worm their way into her flesh, but the jewel kept them at bay. They clawed at her arm, leaving terrible scratches, but they couldn't get under her skin. Their anger prompted more clashes with each other as they realized they had to get farther out of the well to find a victim. They thrashed around, black mist dispelling and re-forming as they fought.

Grace felt her friends grab hold of her ankles as she disappeared almost entirely down the well. She groped around. *There* it was—the Mirrorman's hand among the fiery chaos! Grace's hands clamped onto it.

"Pull us out!" she yelled. The heat was becoming too much, and her skin began to blister.

There were several more unsuccessful pulls, before her hoodie was grabbed in several places and she was wrenched backward, hauling the Mirrorman with her. He collapsed at her feet, unconscious.

At the same moment, Ms. Lemon slid across the floor toward them, with a slender branch twisted around her leg. Another tree branch smashed through the window of the P block, grabbing hold of her arm.

"Girls!" she cried. "Help me!"

Wicked laughter filled the P block, combining eerily with the storm howling outside and the rain pelting through the broken window.

"Bet you're sorry now, Beth," Ms. Gold cackled. "You should have taken *my* side. Now you and Vera can die together."

The more Ms. Lemon struggled, the more the boughs snaked tighter and tighter around her. Through the doorway, Grace could see the formidable Mrs. Quinlan wrapped in tangled branches, unable to move.

Quick as a flash, Adie stretched out her hands, guiding the falling rain into a swirling vortex and throwing it at Ms. Gold. The woman faltered but stayed standing. Adie continued firing watery missiles, hitting her over and over. Grace felt a flurry of air as something invisible rushed past her and knocked over Ms. Gold. Una uncloaked as she rolled away. Jenny used the precious seconds to reproduce her Baskerville hound. It immediately pounced on the teacher's chest. But one vicious strike from Ms. Gold's hands, and the hound was blasted to pieces. The woman then zapped Una and Jenny, sending them flying into the grip of the branches that still held Mrs. Quinlan.

The anarchy of the block seemed suddenly to go quiet as Ms. Gold got slowly to her feet and strolled toward Grace and Adie. Grace shook the Mirrorman's cloak, begging him to come to, but he did not respond. She couldn't see Rachel anywhere, but Adie raised her hands for another water strike.

"Don't bother, little one," the woman said as one of the broken beaded bracelets flew from the ground and snapped itself around Adie's wrists once more. "It's time to answer your true calling."

She nodded toward the well, where two demons had managed to break free from the battle and were crawling across the floor. Ms. Gold smiled as she approached. An ancient, gravelly voice stopped her in her tracks.

"Blond *witch*," the Mirrorman growled, still at Grace's feet. "You'll pay for this."

Grace had seen the look on Ms. Gold's face before—when they had encountered the Mirrorman in the woods. It was genuine fear. But it melted into something defiant.

"You're broken, old man." Her voice trembled. "And I can finish you once and for all!"

Her hands shook as she raised them over him.

"You'll pay..." said a different voice, no longer ancient. "Blond witch!"

Ms. Gold screeched and spun around. Another Mirrorman stood directly in front of her, his weird eyes boring into her face. He didn't look weak at all.

"No!" Tears of fright spilled down Ms. Gold's cheeks.

"You'll. Pay. For. This," he said again, advancing.

As Grace stared aghast at the second Mirrorman, she felt a sharp pain as the fishing fly twisted out of her hand and dropped onto the first Mirrorman's waiting palm. Gripping it in his fist, Grace could feel the wave of energy it sent through him.

"No! You won't stop me now!" Ms. Gold had collected herself and grabbed the second Mirrorman by the collar, but her voice was high-pitched with terror. "I won't let you!"

She dug her nails into his skin, and the Mirrorman

let out a girly squeal. The Glamour spell dissolved, revealing Rachel's porcelain features.

"Ha!" Ms. Gold exclaimed, scraping her clawed hand across Rachel's face, just to be sure. "I taught you well, you little wretch. I taught you *too* well."

Ms. Gold's head nodded with triumph as another beaded bracelet snapped around Rachel's wrists.

"Grace!" Rachel cried.

"*She* can't help you," the woman sneered. "It's over now."

"Yes, it's over." The Mirrorman hoisted himself off the ground and his hands swung like lightning. "For *you!*"

Ms. Gold was hurled to the ground by an unseen force. She slid slowly across the floor to the escaping, crawling demons. She shrieked as they latched on to her with glee, sinking their misty limbs into hers. But they never completed their possession. The Mirrorman pounced, snatching all three into the air and propelling them through the well mouth in a cacophony of hissing squeals. Grace closed her eyes at the disappearing sound of Ms. Gold's screams as she was dragged down into the well.

Another powerful swing of the Mirrorman's arm and the well mouth crunched shut, cutting off the stream of red light and plunging the P block into sudden darkness.

21
back together

The storm was dying down outside and a few rays of moonlight lifted the blackness of the P block. Ms. Lemon was pushing off the branches that bound her. Through the doorway, Grace could hear Mrs. Quinlan snapping at everyone as she, Jenny, and Una unbound their own limbs. Rachel and Adie sat very still nearby, though their beaded bracelets had fallen useless to the floor. The Mirrorman stood motionless by the site of the well. He wasn't the same man who had followed Grace from the past. He looked older—much older—thin, scarred, and tired. She couldn't imagine what he had suffered in his decades down the demon well.

"It was you." Her voice cracked. "In my dreams, in the mirror. It was *you* trying to reach me from inside the well, not the…younger you from the past."

He didn't answer. The jeweled fly had revitalized his body, enough to bring an end to the battle with Ms. Gold, but his face was so weary Grace could hardly bear to look at it.

"You knew who I was," she went on, "when we met in the past. You saw through the Glamour spell."

His eyes dropped to the floor. He slowly turned and made his way to the emergency exit at the end of the block.

"I'm sorry!" Grace called, tears beginning to fall. "I'm so sorry I couldn't stop her from sending you down there!"

He leaned against the door, pushing it open, and fresh, rain-scented air rushed through the hall. He breathed in deeply.

"Wait, Mirrorman—" she started.

He paused to look over his shoulder.

"Bob," he said. "My name's Bob." He gave Grace a nod and then disappeared out into the night.

Jaded and sore, everyone gradually gathered around

the scorched ring that remained at the site of the well. Only Jenny hung back.

"I knew she'd be up to something," Mrs. Quinlan growled, "but this…"

"I'm *so* sorry, girls," Ms. Lemon said. "If I'd have known she meant to use you like this, I might have gone so far as to bind your powers. If only to prevent her interest in you."

"Mrs. Quinlan tried." The words were out of Grace's mouth before she had time to think.

"And how exactly would you know anything about that, Sparky?" the Cat Lady snapped. Grace avoided her gaze.

"Hmph," the woman grunted. "Didn't work anyway—useless Sophrosynic binding."

Grace kept her mouth shut. She figured she would explain that she had broken into Mrs. Quinlan's house and sabotaged the spell when everyone was calm and well rested. In a few weeks. Or months. Or years.

At the sound of gentle sniffling behind them, Rachel rushed to hug Jenny and pull her toward the group.

"Hey," she said softly. "It's okay."

"It's not," Jenny wept. "The hound, Grace. And all that stuff by the river. Then *this*. I'm so sorry."

"It's not your fault." Grace grabbed her in a hug. "She's gone now, and so is her stupid charm. And I'm sorry too—about *that*."

She brushed her fingers over the cut on Jenny's cheek, caused by her slingshot by the river. Jenny smiled.

"Hey, it's the least I deserve."

"Don't be an idiot." Grace wrapped her arms around her friend again, and Rachel, Una, and Adie rushed in for a group hug.

"Oh, for God's sake," Mrs. Quinlan said. "I have to leave or I'm going to throw up."

She marched to the empty doorway and stopped.

"And *you*," she yelled down the hallway. "Teeny girl. Are you going to show your face or what?"

The woman tapped her foot, and Delilah crept around the doorjamb. Mrs. Quinlan coughed.

"Your mother's gone." It was the softest voice Grace had ever heard from Mrs. Quinlan.

Delilah's glance moved from the demon well, to the other girls, and then to Mrs. Quinlan.

"You did well to fetch me and Beth." The woman kept her voice low. "You saved lives."

The girl's face lit up in a happy smile.

"You'll need somewhere to stay," Ms. Lemon said. "But I'm afraid my place is a little small for two."

She looked pleadingly at Mrs. Quinlan, who huffed loudly.

"You like cats?" she snapped at Delilah.

The girl shrugged.

"Well, there's a lot of them. Come on." And Mrs. Quinlan headed off down the hallway, with the small girl scuttling along behind.

"Vera," Ms. Lemon called after her. "What about this mess?"

"School mess," the woman shouted back. "That's for teachers to sort out."

"We can help you clean up, Miss," Una said brightly. "It'll just take a little magic."

"Haven't you learned anything from this, girls?"

Ms. Lemon replied with a sigh. "The practical stuff is far too dangerous. Master your theory first."

"The theory doesn't mean anything without the practical," Rachel said. "We need to learn both—to keep ourselves and others safe."

"You can't take care of us forever, Miss," said Adie gently.

Ms. Lemon looked at each of them.

"You're right," she said. "You've shown me that much already. I'm proud of all of you."

"So?" Una chirped. "Practical lessons from now on!"

"Practical *and* theory," the teacher replied firmly. "No skimping on either, is that clear? And if you fail any theory tests, you lose some spell time. Fair?"

"Fair." Grace smiled.

"Fair for some," Una mumbled. "I hate tests."

Grace fell to the back of the group as Una went into bargaining mode with Ms. Lemon, who rejected every attempt at an alternative to her teaching plan. It felt wonderful to have everyone back together again.

As she passed the broken window, she could see

over the twisted branches to the moonlit night outside. In the puddles left by the storm, she caught the
fleeting reflection of a black-cloaked figure heading
toward the trees, and she smiled. Bob was going
back to his little hut in the woods—and the world
felt like a safer place.

Acknowledgments

I'd like to thank my mom, as always. My siblings, for producing an ever-growing brood of wonderful nieces and nephews (I hope they enjoy these books some day). My dear friend, Rachel Mungra, for being a constant source of amusement and amazement.

About the Author

Erika McGann grew up in Drogheda, Ireland, and now lives in Dublin. She has a respectable job, very normal friends, and rarely dabbles in witchcraft. She loves writing stories that are autobiographical. Sort of.

The Demon Notebook, her first book about Grace and her witch apprentice friends, is also published by Sourcebooks Jabberwocky.

THE DEMON NOTEBOOK

Erika McGann

For Grace and her four best friends, magic is just harmless fun—until it's not...

Things have gone wrong for Grace, Jenny, Rachel, Adie, and Una. Very wrong. A freak snowstorm stranded the whole school, the history teacher's gone bonkers, and their notebook has taken on a diabolical life of its own, bringing all of their previously failed spells to life. At first the girls are thrilled to see their magic finally working.

But the spells are botched and people might get hurt and Una's not acting quite right...

Can the girls stop the madness before the demon notebook works through their list of spells, slowly creeping towards the last, truly awful spell that they didn't really want to happen?

DOROTHY'S DERBY CHRONICLES:

Rise of the Undead Redhead

Meghan Dougherty and Alece Birnbach

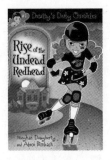

Skating in circles doesn't exactly make you Miss Popular...or does it?

Dorothy Moore has never been outgoing. In fact, she's downright shy. So when she and her sister Sam are forced to move in with their pink-haired, hearse-driving grandma, Dorothy's not sure she can survive as the new kid in school. When she reaches into her gym bag to find her sweats replaced with a sequined spandex body suit courtesy of Grandma Sally, she's sure she won't.

Dorothy just wants to fit in at school, and learning how to skate from Grandma Sally seems like the wrong way to go. But meeting new friends Jade and Gigi—who save Dorothy from super embarrassment—makes all the difference, and Dorothy finds that skating in circles might be the path to happiness and adventure.